THE VERDICT

JAMES PATTERSON is one of the best-known and biggest-selling writers of all time. His books have sold in excess of 325 million copies worldwide and he has been the most borrowed author in UK libraries for the past nine years in a row. He is the author of some of the most popular series of the past two decades – the Alex Cross, Women's Murder Club, Detective Michael Bennett and Private novels – and he has written many other number one bestsellers including romance novels and stand-alone thrillers.

James is passionate about encouraging children to read. Inspired by his own son who was a reluctant reader, he also writes a range of books for young readers including the Middle School, I Funny, Treasure Hunters, House of Robots, Confessions and Maximum Ride series. James is the proud sponsor of the World Book Day Award and has donated millions in grants to independent bookshops. He lives in Florida with his wife and son.

BOOK**SHOTS**

STORIES AT THE SPEED OF LIFE

What you are holding in your hands right now is no ordinary book, it's a BookShot.

BookShots are page-turning stories by James Patterson and other writers that can be read in one sitting.

Each and every one is fast-paced, 100% story-driven; a shot of pure entertainment guaranteed to satisfy.

Available as new, compact paperbacks, ebooks and audio, everywhere books are sold.

BookShots – the ultimate form of storytelling. From the ultimate storyteller.

THE VERDICT

JAMES PATTERSON

WITH *ROBERT GOLD*

BOOK**SHOTS**

1 3 5 7 9 10 8 6 4 2

BookShots
20 Vauxhall Bridge Road
London SW1V 2SA

BookShots is part of the Penguin Random House
group of companies whose addresses can be found at
global.penguinrandomhouse.com

Penguin
Random House
UK

First published by BookShots in 2016

www.penguin.co.uk

A CIP catalogue record for this book is
available from the British Library.

ISBN 9781786530318

Typeset in Garamond Premier Pro font 12/16.5 pt in
India by Thomson Digital Pvt Ltd, Noida Delhi

Printed and bound in Great Britain by Clays Ltd, St Ives Plc

MIX
Paper from
responsible sources
FSC® C018179

Penguin Random House is committed to a sustainable future
for our business, our readers and our planet. This book is made
from Forest Stewardship Council® certified paper.

THE VERDICT

PROLOGUE

THE FLOWERS ON HER dresser had started to wilt, the tightly closed blinds denying them the light they needed to thrive.

The room was kept in darkness.

The chandelier never lit.

The heavy door firmly closed.

The only light came from the television, constantly playing to itself in the corner of the room.

A champagne bottle stood on the table beside her bed. A single glass left, half drunk. Tablets were scattered around the stem.

Her clothes lay strewn across the floor or thrown on the chaise at the foot of her bed, cast off as she fell backwards onto her softly sprung mattress.

From above the bed, her mother looked down on her – her striking face captured in oils. The painting portrayed the strength of character she had both loved and feared.

Without her mother watching over her, she found she could never sleep.

She laid alone, deep in a dream of happiness, oblivious to what others plan.

Silently, the door was opened.

CHAPTER 1

SPRINTING ACROSS THE VAST, manicured Tribeca Hotel lawns, Jon Roscoe wondered to himself if he was getting too old for chasing thugs.

In the late dusk of a midsummer evening, he had seen security images of a man scrambling up the towering wall that surrounds the exclusive property. Immediately he had left his office, run across the hotel's marble foyer, past the Michelin-starred restaurant, through Tribeca's London-gin bar and out of the garden room.

Charging down the sweeping stone staircase that descends from the back of the magnificent building, he saw the man drop down into the immaculately tended flowerbeds, jump quickly to his feet and turn towards the side entrance of the hotel.

Accelerating his pace, Roscoe could see he was gaining on his prey and, as he launched into a flying rugby tackle to drag the man down, he momentarily congratulated himself for maintaining his sprint-fitness. But a second later, as the man landed a surprising blow across the side of his head, knocking him off-balance and giving the man time to leap back to his feet, Roscoe told himself he definitely needed to do more work on his sharpness at the gym in the coming weeks.

Still berating himself for letting his opponent land a punch, Roscoe redoubled his efforts as he attempted to chase the intruder down. His pursuit continued across the lawn, directly towards the luxury hotel.

Open only for the previous three weeks, hundreds of wealthy and influential guests were resident inside the forty floors of exclusive accommodation, as they savoured the ultimate in fine dining and unparalleled levels of comfort and security. A brutal attack on the chairman of the luxury hotel chain, prior to the opening of the London location, had left Roscoe, as Global Head of Security, on high alert and he'd personally committed himself to taking direct charge of the running of the hotel's security for its first six months of operation.

Seeing the man charging straight at the building, Roscoe knew he had to take him down before he could threaten the hotel's inner sanctum.

Hitting his stride, gaining on the man with every step, Roscoe knew this time he wouldn't let him slip.

As he ran towards the ornamental fountain, the man faltered for a split second and Roscoe pounced. Leaping forward onto the man's back, the pair crashed down into the ice-cold water.

Roscoe didn't hesitate.

His ripped six-foot frame overpowered the intruder and he relished submerging him under the freezing water. Grabbing hold of the man's jacket collar, Roscoe dragged him back to the surface, watching him gasp frantically for air.

Then he thrust him back under.

And held him down.

CHAPTER 2

THE INTRUDER'S ARMS FLAILED and his skinny legs thrashed about in the fountain as Roscoe's powerful hands held a vice-like grip on the back of his neck. Increasing the pressure, pushing him down harder, Roscoe forced him under the fountain's hammering water jet.

The man was unable to breathe.

Unflinching, Roscoe held him firmly, knowing he would be desperate for air and would begin to black out as his body was deprived of oxygen.

Only when he felt the man's resistance start to drop was it time to let him surface.

Ripping him from the water, Roscoe tossed the intruder out of the fountain and onto the pristine lawn – throwing him to the ground like the drowned rat he was. Soaked to the skin, his clothes clinging to him, Roscoe climbed from the water after him; standing over his catch, he watched as the man desperately tried to fill his lungs.

Coughing violently, lying prone on the grass, the intruder spluttered up at the Tribeca Hotel's security chief.

'What's wrong with you, Roscoe?' he gasped. 'Have you gone bat-shit? You could have killed me.'

Roscoe said nothing.

Instead he stepped forward, dragged the man to his feet and, holding him with his left hand, shaped to hit him with a sharp right.

'No more, Roscoe, please!' begged the man, half turning away, as he held up his hands to try to protect his face. As he did so, Roscoe dropped his arm, moving quickly to hit him full in the stomach. Folding over in anticipation, the feeble man winced, but before making contact Roscoe grabbed his arm, spun him around like a rag doll and rammed his arm up behind his back.

The man screamed in pain.

'Roscoe!' he yelled. 'I'm sorry – okay, I'm sorry.'

Easing the pressure, Roscoe felt the man relax, before kicking him in the back of the leg and telling him to move.

'One more time, Madison, and I swear I will kill you. You're not welcome here. Get it? This time I'll take you out front, but next time – let's just agree there won't be a next time.'

'There won't be a next time! You've got my word.'

Roscoe had finally lost all patience. This was the third time he had caught Michael Madison trespassing on the grounds of the Tribeca Luxury Hotel in the past seven days. A South African-born investigative journalist working for *The London Informer*, Madison was just one member of the vast contingent of world's press who had spent the last week camped outside the hotel's main entrance. But Madison had constantly crossed the line and, by refusing to recognise the sacrosanct privacy that Tribeca offered to all of its guests, had threatened the very reputation that was Tribeca Luxury Hotels.

The frenetic press fervour on the roads outside the hotel was driven by Tribeca playing host to Harvey Rylands, billionaire businessman and brother-in-law to the current British Prime Minister, Andrew Turner.

And a man on trial for the attempted murder of his lover, Elegant Daniels.

Roscoe knew the world's press had an insatiable appetite for the story. Every global news organisation had stationed a crew outside the main gates, ready to capture the briefest image of Rylands or his wife, Amelia. While the sensational trial was taking place at London's Old Bailey courthouse, the crowd outside the hotel was doubling in number every day, as more and more salacious evidence was presented.

He felt no sympathy for the billionaire. The granting of bail had been almost unprecedented, Rylands' money and contacts no doubt playing a large part. Always accepting that the media had a job to do, and having no desire to be a defender of Harvey Rylands, Roscoe was the protector of the hotel, its reputation and all of its guests. However hard it might be, he was determined to keep the press outside the hotel grounds and its guests safe within.

Marching Michael Madison across the front lawn, past the hotel's towering entrance and down its tree-lined driveway, Roscoe issued his final warning.

'Trespass again and you'll wake up in a hospital bed with a tube coming down your nose. And it won't be me you'll be dealing with; it'll be my old friends from Scotland Yard.'

As an ex-senior officer with London's Metropolitan Police, Roscoe knew it needed only one call from him to have Madison removed from the vicinity, to enjoy a night in an overcrowded jail cell.

'I get it, Roscoe! I promise I do.'

'You'd better,' he replied, pushing Madison forward down the driveway.

Looking ahead, both men stopped dead in their tracks.

'Holy shit!' said Madison, standing motionless as a brand-new Jaguar sports convertible, it headlights on full beam, raced towards the security barrier at the end of the drive.

With no regard for the vast crowd of journalists and onlookers gathered around the entrance, the car increased its speed, sending splintered wood skywards as it crashed through the barrier and accelerated up the main drive.

Standing in the full beam of its headlights, Roscoe could see the car was heading directly for them.

CHAPTER 3

IN A SINGLE, SPLIT-SECOND motion, Roscoe pushed Madison sideways into the garden while hurling himself to the ground, narrowly out of the path of the rapidly approaching vehicle. Lying flat, he watched in amazement as the car veered off the driveway, spun tyre tracks across the lawn, before landing in the flowerbeds at the side of the hotel, where only a few minutes earlier Madison had scrambled over the wall and onto private property.

Turning to look over his shoulder at a startled Madison, Roscoe smiled and said, 'Thank God you weren't any later climbing over that wall or I'd have wasted the rest of my evening picking up tiny pieces of your broken legs.'

But Madison wasn't listening.

Already he was clambering to his feet, searching in his pocket for his camera phone as he did so.

'It's Harvey Rylands!' he exclaimed, quickening his pace as he ran across the driveway and started towards the smashed car.

'Don't even think it!' cried Roscoe, instantly coming after him. 'This is still Tribeca Hotel's private property, and you're still trespassing.'

'The man might need help,' said Madison, gesturing towards the car.

'I'm pretty certain he won't want any help from you,' said Roscoe, placing his hands on Madison's shoulders and turning him back towards the entrance gates. 'But don't worry, I'll make sure he gets the best possible attention. Now, get out!'

Dismissing Madison, Roscoe saw the world's press eagerly make their way onto the hotel grounds and begin a charge in the direction of the car. Competition between camera crews was already taking place as they vied for the best video footage of the crushed vehicle, while photojournalists lit up the hotel driveway as pictures were rapidly snapped, ready to be raced around the world a second later.

Roscoe urgently called to his assistant, Stanley Samson, who on hearing the crash had hurriedly come out of the front of the hotel.

'We need the main gates closing now,' shouted Roscoe, referring to the soaring 'Tribeca Luxury Hotels'-inscribed gates, kept open at most times to allow guests unencumbered access in and out of the property. 'And get all of these press guys back out front, and keep them there,' he added, rapidly making his way across the ploughed lawn to the stranded car, where steam was pouring from its front grille.

Quickly following his boss's instructions, Roscoe heard Stanley shout at the front gate security team to stop all access, followed by a heavy groan from the press pack as they were swiftly moved back behind the closing gates.

As he approached the wrecked vehicle, he was amazed to see its driver's side door swing open and the ample figure of its driver roll himself out of the tight cockpit. Pushing away the deployed airbag, Harvey Rylands extricated himself from the car, before staggering onto the lawn and swaying from side to side in a non-existent breeze.

What a toad! thought Roscoe, as a ruddy-faced Rylands, clearly the worse for a considerable amount of drink, gingerly took uncertain steps towards him. 'Good evening, Mr Rylands, welcome back,' he called as Rylands approached. 'Can I get you any medical attention?'

'I'm fine, just fine,' growled Rylands, waving his arms as he stumbled across the grass. 'If it wasn't for those bastards, I'd have had a clear run. The flashing cameras disorientated me – their fault entirely.'

'Of course it was, sir,' said Roscoe, offering Rylands a steadying arm, his only aim being to get the billionaire businessman back inside the hotel with the smallest possible amount of fuss.

'Will you . . . ?' Rylands stopped, searching for words in his alcohol-fuelled state. 'The car. Will you deal with the car? Get it repaired. If you could have it back out front by morning, it would be greatly appreciated,' he said.

Unlikely, thought Roscoe, but he would worry about that later.

Only as Rylands turned to face him was Roscoe hit by the full force of the alcohol on his breath. As he took an unintended step backwards, Rylands hollered at him.

'As I said, their fault entirely. They're scum, out to destroy me.'

Roscoe thought Rylands was doing a pretty good job of that himself, but simply nodded his head as the billionaire turned towards the closed gate, bellowing at the top of his Old Etonian voice as he did.

'Why don't you fuck off, you miserable fuckers, you bloodthirsty gannets! When all this is over, I'm going to sue every single fucking one of you.'

CHAPTER 4

LYING IN HER BED in her small South London apartment, Jessie Luck reflected on the testimony she had heard during the previous week. Never had she dreamed she would be invited to take a seat on a jury passing judgment on a defendant with as high a profile as Harvey Rylands.

London's Old Bailey courthouse could be an intimidating place, even for the most seasoned legal professional. At the age of seventy-three, when she had walked into a courtroom for the very first time, Jessie had felt both a little anxious and slightly overwhelmed by the whole experience. Telling herself each day that she was undertaking her civic duty, she made every effort to consider each piece of evidence as it was presented to the jury.

On the opening day of the trial she had stared up in awe at the beautiful hand-painted ceilings as she entered through the court's domed Grand Hall. Inside the chamber she had looked at the imposing wood-panelled walls and imagined all of the criminals who, over the past century, had stood in the dock ready to face British justice.

'Not guilty' was the plea she had heard Rylands enter, as he stood in the dock for the first time. While the allegations against him were read to the court, she had watched as he had stood impassively, showing no emotion even when the charge of 'Attempted murder' was levelled at him.

In November of the previous year, Rylands was accused of entering the home of Elegant Daniels in the dead of night, to carry out the most brutal attack imaginable as she slept alone in her bed.

From the evidence Jessie had heard, she knew that Rylands and Elegant Daniels were lovers. To Jessie, it seemed as though all sides accepted this as fact, but the prosecution team still spent what she felt were unnecessary hours trawling through the most intimate details of their relationship. Personal and invasive evidence had shown conclusively that the couple had been together in Elegant's bed earlier in the evening on the night of the attack.

Jessie believed what happened next was critical to the case.

Footage from security cameras in the parking lot close to Elegant Daniels' home, and regularly used by Rylands, showed his car leaving soon after 1 a.m.

Footage from a little after 3 a.m. appeared to show his car returning.

Mrs Jefferies, the prosecuting barrister, presented this as defining evidence. But as far as Jessie could see, with the parking-lot lights extinguished, it was impossible to identify the car, let alone whether Harvey Rylands was driving it. Jessie liked Mrs Jefferies and trusted her clear approach and honest face, and wondered if perhaps she should give her the benefit of the doubt. If Harvey Rylands had returned to the parking garage close to Elegant Daniels' home in the middle of the night, it was hard for Jessie to believe he wasn't guilty of the attack.

And then came the evidence of how Elegant Daniels had been savagely attacked in her own bed. This would keep Jessie awake for weeks, maybe even months to come. As she reached across to turn out the lamp that had stood on her bedside table for the past twenty years, she decided she would keep her light on a little longer, or at least until she heard her adopted son, Jon, return home for the night.

To be attacked at her most vulnerable.

Attacked in a place where everyone needed to feel safe.

A pillow thrust over her face; held down, to stop her breathing.

Jessie hated even to imagine the fear.

The plan had been to suffocate the woman. Instead, Elegant Daniels had been rendered unconscious – but alive.

Unable to defend herself, she had been at the mercy of her attacker.

In the pitch black, he had launched his sadistic assault.

Closing her eyes, Jessie could still see the horrific evidential photographs, at times almost too graphic to bear, which she had forced herself to review.

Drawing a knife, her attacker had cut away each eyeball, very precisely uprooting them from their sockets.

And in their place he had left two shining, blood-red rubies.

CHAPTER 5

FIFTEEN MINUTES AFTER HER husband's dramatic return to London's Tribeca Luxury Hotel, Amelia Rylands pulled her own sports car into the employee parking lot at the rear of the building. With no desire to fight her way through the world's press, she'd arranged private access with the hotel's security team through a staff entrance for the entirety of her stay.

Exhausted, both physically and mentally, after another day devoted to her unswerving support of her husband at the Old Bailey, she had spent most of the evening in conference with his legal team, reviewing the day's evidence while assisting in the planning of the defence team's strategy for the following day. At times she felt certain that, hidden amongst all the reams of paper and box files, there was one tiny piece of evidence waiting to exonerate Harvey and set him free.

Throughout the meeting she had watched her husband steadily drink himself into oblivion, but had felt too drained to contemplate a confrontation.

She had seen it so many times before.

Whenever Harvey failed to get his own way, couldn't enforce his will or his money simply wouldn't buy him the result he wanted, he turned to drink. Seeking confrontation, he would become more and more aggressive.

Tonight, too tired to fight, Amelia had ignored him, only for a blazing row to explode between him and his lead counsel, culminating in Harvey storming from the meeting to drive himself back to the Tribeca Hotel.

Walking through the rear entrance, she was pleased to be greeted by the foyer manager, Anna Conquest. Amelia had met Anna at the start of the previous week and had instantly engaged with her. Anna had offered help with every possible detail and had done everything within her power to make Amelia's stay at Tribeca as painless as possible; she had, in short, been the consummate professional. Anna smiled when she saw Amelia approaching, and Amelia couldn't help but respond.

'Mrs Rylands, welcome back. I won't ask if you've had a good day, but I do hope it has been tolerable.'

'Thank you, Anna,' she replied, taking hold of Anna's proffered hand and sitting with her for a moment on one of the sumptuous sofas that line all Tribeca hallways.

'Is there anything I can get for you?' asked Anna, showing genuine concern.

'No, I'm fine. A tough day in court, but at least I get to come back here in the evening. Has my husband made an appearance?'

Anna gently raised her eyebrows.

'Tell me what that means,' said Amelia, trying to raise a smile.

'His car overran the driveway when he returned to the hotel; might have picked up a few scratches, but nothing that can't be fixed.'

Tribeca members of staff are taught to be nothing if not discreet.

'But he's okay?' she asked.

'Absolutely fine. He went straight up to your suite.'

'I'm sure everyone at the hotel will be glad when this is all over and my husband and I are long departed,' said Amelia. 'And if you're not glad to see the back of us, I'm sure you'll be ready to say farewell to the press camped outside the front gates. I know I will be!'

'You shouldn't let them get to you. I don't think we even notice them,' said Anna.

'You're too good!' said Amelia, clapping her hands. 'I'm sure you do notice them, and after today's evidence they'll be having a field day. The prosecution spent endless hours working through every sordid fact they could rake up. The samples of Harvey's hair they'd taken from Ms Daniels' bed, the traces of his saliva they'd found along with his semen on the bed sheets. They couldn't have made it more humiliating if they tried.'

They sat in silence until Amelia continued, 'Harvey lost his rag, exploded at his counsel this evening. Of course he'd been drinking too much – that's his way – but he couldn't understand why the case wasn't moving forward. We all know Harvey was having an affair with Ms Daniels – he's a womaniser; he can't help himself. I've known that for years, but surely that isn't evidence of a crime?'

'No,' said Anna, shaking her head.

It occurred to Amelia how little Anna's job had to do with hotel services, but in reality veered from counselling to surrogate friendship, or simply providing a shoulder to cry on.

Amelia felt she needed all three.

'I can't bear to think what the papers will say tomorrow and, no doubt, the news channels tonight. We certainly make great copy. We've been married for over twenty years and my guess is he's cheated on me in nineteen of those.'

Amelia could see the look in Anna's eyes, but she didn't want her pity.

'Hey, I married him; should have known what I was letting myself in for. And the good thing about an old dog like Harvey is that he always comes home in the end.'

Giving Anna a wink, Amelia squeezed her hand, before getting to her feet.

'I must keep positive. As they say: tomorrow always is another day,' she smiled. 'Thanks for listening.'

Standing next to her guest, Anna asked once again if there was anything she could get Mrs Rylands.

'A new husband perhaps?' Amelia laughed forlornly. 'Do you think I'm stupid, Anna, standing by him?'

'That's not for me to say, Mrs Rylands. Nobody knows what goes on inside a marriage.'

Amelia looked at Anna.

'I love him, and I don't believe he tried to kill her,' she said. 'And even if he did, however hard I tried, I don't think I'd stop loving him. Guess that makes me like those crazy women on the daytime talk-shows – in love with a killer.'

'I don't think so, Mrs Rylands.'

'He's got a horrendous temper – everyone could see that tonight – but I can't abandon him now. He needs me, even if I do sometimes wonder what would happen if he really lost control again.'

Amelia stepped away, before turning back and looking at Anna.

'Perhaps I'll be next.'

CHAPTER 6

ROSCOE RIPPED OFF HIS sodden clothes as he entered the security control room, two floors beneath the hotel's main lobby, then kicked off the shoes Harvey Rylands had vomited all over as he escorted him back to his suite. Anger still boiled within him at Rylands' behaviour.

While he accepted that Rylands was a high-profile guest of Tribeca Hotels, he felt his actions were threatening to tarnish the chain's global reputation. Rylands' conduct in and around the hotel grew worse each day. Roscoe didn't care if he was guilty or not, he just wanted him gone.

Every day the media feasted on the Rylands trial, and every day it became harder and harder for the hotel to ensure that its incomparable levels of service were enjoyed by each and every one of its guests at the London location. Roscoe feared the hotel's reputation would be dragged down alongside Rylands.

Reaching for the dry T-shirt he had left hanging on the back of one of the office chairs, Roscoe turned as the security-room door opened and Anna walked in. He had known Anna for the past two years, having worked with her first briefly at Tribeca's luxury hotel in Edinburgh, before she joined the team to prepare for the grand opening of the new Mayfair hotel. He quickly pulled the T-shirt over his head as she came in, carrying two cups of coffee.

'I thought you might need this to warm you through,' she said, handing him a cup.

'You're a life-saver. How old do you have to be before you're too old for fighting in fountains?'

Anna laughed as Roscoe rested on the corner of his desk, watching her seat her delicate figure opposite him. He couldn't help but notice that she'd pulled her long, dark hair back away from her face and for a moment had to stop himself staring. As she talked, he realised she reminded him in many ways of his estranged wife.

He turned away.

'I bumped into Amelia Rylands,' she continued.

'I don't want to hear any more about that family,' said Roscoe, getting up from his desk to pace the room.

'They're our guests.'

'He threw up all over my favourite shoes.'

'Poor Jon,' she teased. 'Amelia's having a tough time of it.'

'She's meant to be. Her husband's on trial for attempted murder.'

'I think she might be scared of him.'

'Nobody's making her stand by him or go to court every day, or face the press and suffer through the evidence. It is her choice. She could've walked away, but I guess a billion-dollar fortune is a tough tie to break.'

'Twenty years is a long time. You can't choose who you fall in love with.'

Sitting back down on the edge of his desk, Roscoe folded his arms. His wife Marika was the only woman he had ever really loved, yet she was currently living more than four hundred miles away with their twin daughters, and he hated it.

'You really think she's scared of him?' he said.

'She's married to a bully who's used to buying his way out of whatever scrapes he gets himself into.'

'This is a bit more than a scrape.'

'True. Perhaps that means he can't buy his way out of this one, which is why he ends up taking it out on her. She says she loves him, but I'm not sure I'd still love a man if I thought he'd done what Harvey Rylands is accused of.'

'And yet each night she goes back to the suite with him.'

'Then I just hope she's safe.'

'So do I,' said Roscoe, looking under his desk for an old pair of trainers, 'but she's made her own choices. Guilty or not, she'd be better off without him. He's one big fraud. The whole thing with the Prime Minister – Rylands couldn't trade more heavily on it if he tried. And it's not even as if he really is the PM's brother-in-law.'

'He's not?'

'It was Rylands' first wife, Barbara Turner, who was the PM's half-sister. When she died, Harvey inherited her family fortune. He's been free to embarrass the Prime Minister ever since – arrested in Kuwait, falling flat on the cobbled stones outside Number Ten Downing Street, a great ambassador for Britain!'

'And now he's thrown up over your favourite shoes!' Anna smiled at him. 'Come on, let's get you a stronger drink and get you out of this mood.'

Roscoe sighed. 'I'd love one, but I've got to collect Martin from the station.'

'Rain check,' said Anna, getting to her feet. 'The coffee will have to keep you warm for now.'

'Anna,' said Roscoe as she headed for the door. 'What made you think Mrs Rylands is scared?'

Anna paused and looked across at Roscoe.

'Hearing her say that, however hard she tried, she couldn't stop loving him.'

CHAPTER 7

THE SKY CRACKED AND a summer storm hit as Roscoe parked his car outside London's King's Cross Station. It was close to midnight, yet crowds were still milling around the surrounding streets and he watched as late-night revellers huddled together under whatever cover they could find to shelter from the torrential downpour.

Roscoe stopped in the same place he always did when meeting his adopted son, Martin. Martin running track for his school team meant that Roscoe was used to late-night pickups during the summer months, with the team often catching the last train back from national events. Even though Martin had just celebrated his fifteenth birthday, Roscoe always tried to meet him in person, not wanting him travelling the Underground network late at night.

His watch told him it was five minutes after midnight. The train from Cambridge had been due in a minute before twelve, and he recognised some of Martin's track teammates heading out of the station. But he didn't see Martin amongst them. Assuming he was straggling at the back, probably chatting to one of the girls, Roscoe gave it five minutes more. At ten minutes after twelve, with the rain still bouncing off the windows of his SUV, he decided to run into the station and drag Martin back to the car.

As he hurried across the plaza at the front of the station, Roscoe realised he was getting soaked to the skin for the second time that evening. He dashed inside the cavernous station, where the last trains of the day were pulling in.

Looking around the open space, there was no sign of Martin.

He ran his hands through his close-cropped blond hair to try and dry it off once again, then made his way over to platform eight where the Cambridge train had pulled in.

'Hey, Mr Roscoe,' called across one of Martin's track teammates.

'Hi, George, you seen Martin anywhere?'

'Martin?' said the boy, clearly stalling.

'Yeah, you know the one – just over six feet tall, black hair, quite skinny,' said Roscoe.

'Yeah . . . Martin didn't come to the meet today.'

'He didn't?' said Roscoe, not trying to hide his surprise.

'No, I think he was off sick.'

Roscoe looked at the boy.

'He didn't come to school this morning, either.'

'Didn't he?'

The boy started to back away. 'I gotta go, Mr Roscoe. My mum's waiting,' he said, as he turned to exit.

'Hold on, George. Have you heard from Martin at all today?' Roscoe walked across to him, but the boy said nothing and Roscoe could tell he was weighing up betraying a confidence against telling him the truth. 'I need to know, as right now I've no idea where Martin is.'

'He messaged me this morning saying he wasn't at school today, and not to try and get in touch with him,' George said reluctantly. 'That's all I know.' He looked over to the exit, where his mother was standing. 'Sorry, Mr Roscoe, I've really gotta go.'

Standing alone in the wide-open space, Roscoe watched as George threw his kit bag over his shoulder and ran towards her. Scanning every corner of the station, he wanted to believe Martin would step out of the shadows at any second.

As a parent, he was hoping.

But as a former member of London's Metropolitan Police, he knew that wasn't going to happen.

Fear poured through his body.

Martin was missing.

CHAPTER 8

ROSCOE SCANNED THE STATION one more time, before reaching for his phone and calling Martin.

The call went straight to voicemail.

'Martin's phone. Can't talk. Leave a message. Bye!'

Always straight to the point, thought Roscoe.

'Martin, it's your dad. Where are you? Call me.'

As he walked back through the now almost-empty station, Roscoe continued to look for Martin, but knew he wasn't there. He couldn't remember a day in the past fifteen years when he hadn't known exactly where Martin was, and now, without warning, he was gone.

Roscoe was terrified.

In adopting his sister's child, Roscoe had always loved Martin as his own son, while letting him remember who his mother was. At times he wondered if he over-compensated, especially in the early years when his house had resembled the world's biggest toy shop. But Martin had grown up to be a great kid, and Roscoe knew Amanda would have been proud.

Amanda had given birth to Martin when she was only seventeen years old. The secret of Martin's biological father was one she chose never to reveal, and on the day she brought her son home to the house she shared with her brother, Roscoe had become the father figure in Martin's life.

He could never have imagined, though, that in less than eighteen months, with Martin no more than a tiny toddler, he would become the sole parent to such a young child. Out celebrating her nineteenth birthday, Amanda was attacked on her way home. Struck on the head from behind, savagely beaten, she was left comatose at the roadside.

It was four days before Christmas.

Six days later, on December 27th, Roscoe made the impossible decision to switch off her life support.

Her killer was never caught.

As he climbed back into his car, Roscoe's mobile buzzed.

His heart racing, he grabbed for the phone.

A message from Martin.

'Sorry I missed the train, Dad. Great race, came in second.'

CHAPTER 9

ROSCOE HELD THE PHONE in his hand and stared at the message.

Relief washed over him. Martin was safe.

But he was lying.

First off, he needed to know where his son was. He called his number.

The phone rang and Martin picked up.

'Hey, Dad, how you doing?'

Hearing his son's voice, tears welled in Roscoe's eyes. Wiping them away with his hand, he found himself unable to speak.

'Dad, you there?'

Roscoe looked out of his car window at the increasingly deserted station, still illuminated by the London night-time lights. He inhaled deeply.

'I'm here, son. Where are you?'

'I'm sorry, Dad. I got a ride back with one of the coaches. I know I should've called you. Then we got caught up in traffic, but we're on the move now. I'll be home in thirty minutes.'

Roscoe couldn't say anything.

'Dad? Is that okay?'

'That's great, son, I'm glad you're on your way. See you in half an hour.'

Roscoe just wanted his son home.

'Bye, Dad.'

'Love you,' said Roscoe.

'Love you, too.'

Martin disconnected the phone.

Only the incredible help and wisdom of his own wonderful Aunt Jessie had given Roscoe the confidence to care for and adopt Martin, at a time when he was a rookie cop and still only a young man of twenty-two. Becoming a single parent of an eighteen-month-old boy was an incredible challenge but with Aunt Jessie only a flight of stairs away, he was never alone.

Jessie had raised Roscoe from the age of five, after cancer had cruelly stolen away his own mother. She had stepped in without a moment's hesitation and suddenly her own family, of herself and her teenage son Alvin, had doubled in size. Jon and Amanda had become part of her family and, from the moment he adopted Martin, he knew Aunt Jessie remained the mainstay of his.

The first time Roscoe had brought Marika home to meet Jessie and Martin, he knew they'd fallen for her quiet charm and wonderful humour almost as much as he had. Her disarming natural beauty drew people to her. Marriage followed and then their own twin daughters, but Martin was as much a part of that new family as any one of them.

Roscoe had continued to do his level best to give his son the greatest possible opportunities in life, teaching him right from wrong, helping him make his way in the world.

Whenever his son needed to talk, he was there.

They didn't have secrets.

Until now.

CHAPTER 10

THE STORM CLOUDS HAD cleared the next morning, leaving a bright sun shining through the windows of the red London bus and onto the face of Jessie Luck as she journeyed back to the Old Bailey courthouse to hear the next day of evidence in the Harvey Rylands trial.

As the judge brought the court to order, Jessie looked across from the jury box at Mrs Jefferies reviewing her papers. Closing her folder, Mrs Jefferies rose to her feet and called her final witness for the prosecution.

'Your Honour, the prosecution calls Ms Elegant Daniels.'

An audible gasp ran across the court, and Jessie could feel the buzz of anticipation as she joined each of her fellow jurors in turning towards the entrance to the hundred-year-old chamber.

The doors opened and, following a moment's pause, Jessie saw the gracefully tall and strikingly beautiful Elegant Daniels step into the courtroom, escorted on the arm of an usher. *Never has a woman's name been a truer reflection of herself*, thought Jessie.

Dressed in a fitted black suit, her hair pulled tightly back from her face and wearing the darkest of dark glasses, Elegant Daniels tapped her white stick against the wooden benches that lined the courtroom, as hesitantly she made her way towards the witness box.

Taking the stand, she briefly stumbled, before regaining her composure as her gloved hand gripped the side of the witness box. Jessie watched as Elegant Daniels appeared momentarily disorientated, unsure of which way to turn until, on hearing the judge's voice, the victim was able to compose herself and moved to face him.

Listening intently as Elegant Daniels took her oath in a faltering voice, Jessie found it impossible to draw her eyes away from the majestic woman who now appeared so damaged. Only when Jessie saw her standing alone in the witness box was she struck by the tragic enormity of what had befallen her.

Her hand shaking on the ancient Bible, the witness swore that the evidence she would give would be the truth, the whole truth and nothing but the truth. When offered a seat, she simply expressed her preference to remain standing and, as Mrs Jefferies spoke, Elegant Daniels slowly turned her face towards her.

'Ms Daniels, may I begin by conveying the court's appreciation to you for making what must have been an incredibly difficult personal journey to be with us here today.'

Elegant nodded slowly in a show of appreciation, and Jessie found herself continuing to scrutinise the beautiful woman who stood, so vulnerable, before the court. She couldn't begin to comprehend the pain and suffering she must have endured since she was attacked.

'The court has heard, from a number of your neighbours,' continued Mrs Jefferies, 'that a violent argument took place in your home shortly before one in the morning on the night you were attacked. Can you tell us if such an argument took place between you and the defendant?'

'It did,' Elegant confirmed, her voice strengthening.

'And may I ask you as to its nature?'

'Subsequent to our love-making, the defendant stepped from my bed, informing me he was returning home to his wife.'

'How did you respond?'

'I felt used. I said I wasn't going to be treated in that way any longer. We'd discussed his leaving his wife before; I thought he'd been genuine. I believed we were planning a life together, so this time I gave him an ultimatum. If he wanted to see me again, he had to be with me permanently.'

'And how did he respond?'

'He exploded into what I can only describe as a terrifying rage. I'd never seen him like that before, there was such anger. I knew he had a temper, but he'd never directed it at me in such a manner. He roared at me, and told me I couldn't issue him with an ultimatum. Then he accused me of blackmailing him. Harvey . . .' Elegant Daniels paused to correct herself, 'the defendant appeared to be out of control. I didn't know the man who was standing in my bedroom. I was terrified.'

Turning directly to the court she continued, 'He raised his hand, balled a fist and went to strike me.'

CHAPTER 11

'AND DID HE HIT you?' asked Mrs Jefferies, renewing her examination after an audible gasp from the packed courtroom.

'No.'

Elegant Daniels waited, holding the court's rapt attention.

'Running from the bedroom, I avoided his blow. Then I started screaming. I imagine that's what my neighbours heard. I screamed at him to leave, screamed for him to get out of my home. Eventually he did.'

'And after that, Ms Daniels?'

'I was shaking. I walked into the living room, poured myself a glass of whisky and drank it straight down. I then returned to my bedroom, dressed in my nightclothes and went to bed.'

Jessie looked across at the witness stand and wondered where Elegant Daniels found such composure in giving her evidence. After the horrors Elegant had endured, Jessie admired her strength enormously but, at the same time, struggled to imagine her as a friend. Jessie pictured herself baking a fudge cake in her kitchen, smothered in chocolate, but somehow it was impossible to see Elegant Daniels calling in for a slice of cake and a cup of tea. Jessie smiled at the thought of the witness sitting at her kitchen table, and then immediately reprimanded herself as she realised she had become momentarily distracted.

Quickly returning her attention to Mrs Jefferies, Jessie heard the prosecutor ask Elegant at what point, on the night of the attack, she had first become aware of an intruder in her home. Making Jessie believe this was the story she had come to tell, in preparation for her answer, Elegant Daniels edged her hands around the witness box until she was almost directly facing the jury.

'I was in a deep sleep. In spite of everything that had gone before, it was a restful one – probably the last I will ever enjoy. I always kept a very dark bedroom, tightly shuttered, the door firmly closed.

'I felt a breath upon my face.

'And then another, followed by the almost imperceptible feeling of someone caressing my cheek. I was terrified.

'Was I awake?

'My heart was racing, but I felt frozen with fear.

'In the darkness I was blind.

'Closer and closer came the breath.

'And then I felt a touch upon my skin.

'I hurled myself forward. Screaming; screaming in terror, crying for help.'

Elegant Daniels raised her voice, sharing her desperation with the captivated courtroom.

'I could never have imagined the pain of a fist hitting me full in the face would be so great.

'I was thrown backwards as a hand was clasped across my mouth.

'I was hit again.

'This time harder. The punch carried such anger.

'I tried. I tried . . .'

Jessie heard a break in Elegant Daniels' voice. In unison with the rest of the court, she held her breath.

'I tried to wrestle myself free, but my attacker's strength was too great. I remember a pillow being placed over my face.

'I couldn't breathe.

'I kicked out.

'I tried again to scream.

'And then I was gone.'

Mrs Jefferies let the courtroom compose itself before she continued.

'Thank you, Ms Daniels. I realise this is incredibly difficult, but I have to ask you to take us a little further. You lost consciousness?'

'I believe so.'

'You woke a number of hours later, at some time around seven the following morning?'

'That's correct.'

'Again, I realise how difficult this is for you, but could you share with the court what you discovered?'

Looking at Elegant Daniels, Jessie watched her inhale deeply as she struggled to regain her composure.

Raising a hand to the side of her face, she continued.

'The searing pain running through my head told me I was alive. I felt my face, but even in the darkness I knew. Instinctively, I reached to turn on a light, but as I did so, the blackest of nights remained.

'I touched the blood running down my face – the only tears I could cry.

'My eyes had been gouged from my face.'

Mrs Jefferies paused for a moment, then asked, 'Ms Daniels, do you have any way of identifying your attacker?'

Turning her face to where she believed the defendant was standing in the dock at the rear of the court, she whispered, 'His smell. His sour breath. His heavy touch. I knew him instantly.'

As she spoke, Elegant Daniels moved her hand from her face, and as she did so she swiftly removed her dark glasses.

'He left me for dead,' she proclaimed, pointing her finger towards where she knew he was sitting. 'It was him – the defendant, Harvey Rylands.'

Jessie heard cries of horror from across the courtroom and looked back towards the witness box.

Standing motionless, Elegant Daniels had exposed her hollowed eyes to the court.

CHAPTER 12

CLASPING HER HAND ACROSS her mouth, Jessie felt a wave of shock and dismay sweep across the courtroom. Now, witness to the extreme suffering of Elegant Daniels, she found it almost impossible to imagine the agony the victim must have endured. Finally, as the court began to quiet, the ever-calm Judge Phillips raised his hand to indicate the need for silence. Asking Ms Daniels if she would mind replacing her glasses, he brought the court to order.

Turning to the prosecuting barrister, Mrs Jefferies, he sought assurances that none of the theatrics were her doing and, once such an assurance was given, the trial was set to continue.

In Jessie's mind, Elegant Daniels had succeeded in raising sympathy for herself, while simultaneously increasing the jury's hostility towards Harvey Rylands, in the most dramatic way possible.

For the defence, Humphrey Adams, QC, took to his feet.

'Ms Daniels, allow me to echo my learned friend in thanking you for your attendance at court today and in recognising the horrific attack you have suffered – and which we have all now witnessed.'

Still standing, Elegant Daniels offered no acknowledgement.

'We've heard much about the supposed state of Mr Rylands' marriage,' said Mr Adams.

Jessie glanced in the direction of Amelia Rylands, who sat stoically in her seat as she listened to her husband's lover offer her testimony.

'But may I ask you about your own marriage?' Mr Adams asked.

'I have never been married.'

'No, never married,' Mr Adams replied hesitantly, consulting his brief. 'That's right, but nonetheless never short of gentleman callers, would I be right in saying?' He quickly continued, looking up from his papers and addressing the jury directly. 'Or, to put it another way, a different man in your bed every night – any one of whom might have carried out this horrifying attack upon you?'

Jessie noticed Mrs Jefferies about to raise an objection, before she detected a short sigh followed by a raised eyebrow from Judge Phillips, as he interceded on what he regarded as Mr Adams' inappropriate line of questioning.

'Apologies, Your Honour,' said the defence counsel, before resuming his cross-examination. 'May I ask you, Ms Daniels, do you work?'

'I have various sources of income.'

'So we could say you are gainfully employed?' Mr Adams probed, removing his spectacles.

'I receive a number of different incomes.'

'Was the defendant, Mr Rylands, one of your sources of income? Before you answer,' said Mr Adams, flicking through his papers, 'there is a record here of a number of transfers from Mr Rylands' bank account to your own. June the fourteenth, six thousand pounds; June the twenty-second, three thousand pounds; June the thirtieth, three thousand pounds.' Raising his voice, Mr Adams turned to face the jury, 'July the fourteenth, nine thousand pounds. That must have been quite a night.'

'They were gifts,' Elegant Daniels replied. Jessie heard a crack in her voice as the witness rallied to try and defend her position.

'Did you receive so-called "gifts" from many other gentlemen callers?'

Elegant Daniels did not respond.

'You may answer,' said the judge.

But Mr Adams was continuing his cross-examination.

'How did you meet Harvey Rylands, Ms Daniels?'

'I was introduced to him at a cocktail party I was attending with my former lover,' she whispered.

'May I ask who that was?'

A long silence followed. Then Elegant Daniels looked up and spoke in a strong, clear voice.

'His brother-in-law. Andrew Turner, the Prime Minister.'

CHAPTER 13

ROSCOE WAS SITTING WITH Anna in the private office at the rear of the foyer of the London Tribeca Luxury Hotel. They were both transfixed by the events of the day as they unfolded on the television news reports that ran repeatedly throughout the day – as was the whole nation.

'Questions to the Prime Minister,' had been the call from the Speaker of the House, as Andrew Turner stood at the dispatch box in the House of Commons to face the toughest thirty minutes of his political career. Challenged directly on his involvement with Elegant Daniels, of how he too had used her as a paid-for lover, he refused to comment on matters currently taking place at the Old Bailey.

Roscoe struggled to think of a day in recent British history when such sensational news dominated the headlines. Smiling, he thought of his Aunt Jessie being at the very centre of the action.

'I don't think it will faze her in the slightest,' he said to Anna, when she asked him how he thought Jessie would be coping. 'I know her legs are a bit stiff from sitting in the jury box each day, but it takes a lot to shake her. She couldn't care less what the Prime Minister's been up to; she'll just want to get to the truth.'

'You must've spoken to her about the case a little bit?'

'I promise: not a word. I've hardly seen her since she was selected for the jury. She's got her own front door, so she's very much doing her own thing while the trial is on. I saw her for five minutes last night, but other than that we haven't spoken.'

'What was last night?' said Anna, kicking off her high-heeled shoes and edging down the volume on the latest reporter standing outside the Houses of Parliament.

'Martin was last night,' said Roscoe.

'You're worried about him?' asked Anna, rubbing her feet, having been on them for the past eight hours.

Roscoe nodded.

'Something's going on with him, but I don't know what.'

'What kind of something?' asked Anna, as Roscoe slid his size-eleven foot across the floor, settling it next to hers.

'What size feet have you got?'

'Size three,' she laughed, her tiny foot up against his.

'And just how tall are you, now you've got your shoes off?'

'Five foot three-and-a-half inches, if you must know. Good things come in small packages.'

'They do indeed,' said Roscoe, smiling as he lazed back into the luxurious sofa.

'So what's the "something" with Martin?' said Anna, tucking her legs up on the sofa beside him. 'If you don't tell me, how am I supposed to share my mother's Scottish wisdom with you?'

'I'm sure you've much wisdom to share,' said Roscoe, 'but if I'm being honest, I don't really know. We've always had a great relationship; even when Marika and the girls came along, Martin and I always shared everything. Or at least I thought we did.' He hesitated. 'He lied to me about where he was yesterday, for the whole day. He skipped school and then put on a pretence of going to a track meet, but I know he wasn't there. For a while I had no idea where he was.'

'Did you ask him?'

'I'm still hoping he'll tell me when he's ready.' Roscoe looked directly into Anna's dark eyes. 'When he was missing I didn't care what he was up to. I just wanted him home.'

He dropped his head forward, and Anna ran her hand through his short cropped hair.

He looked up at her.

'What am I doing, Anna? I've got Martin going who-knows-where; the two most beautiful twin daughters in the world live four hundred miles away, and all I can do is Skype-call them each evening. That's not being a good dad.'

'You're being stupid. You're a great dad – but nobody said it was easy.'

'They were right.'

Impulsively, he leaned across and placed his hand on her arm, pulling her closer into a kiss. He felt her breath shorten as he moved his hand across her body.

And then his phone buzzed.

Laughing, they moved apart, and Roscoe took the phone from his pocket.

'I've got to take this. It's a VIP line.'

CHAPTER 14

STEPPING OUT OF A black London taxicab, Jessie Luck imagined herself already inside her apartment, savouring a cup of tea with her feet resting on her old sofa. As she struggled through her front door, try as she might, she couldn't ever remember her legs aching like this.

The Prime Minister and Elegant Daniels?

She still couldn't quite bring herself to believe it. But why make it up? And after everything she'd been through, why would Elegant Daniels invite further interrogation into her life?

Jessie knew Andrew Turner was a man who was protected in many different ways. She had talked in the past with Jon about the influence and access that powerful figures demand, of the contacts that allowed them another way of life and different moral standards.

She wondered how far protection of the Prime Minister went. Did it include attempting to have someone killed? She'd watched too many movies with Martin, she told herself. This wasn't James Bond. But what did happen, the night Elegant Daniels was blinded?

The moment she finally did sit down she let out an exhausted sigh. Plumping her cushion and turning on her radio, all she wanted to do was drink her tea and start the next chapter in her latest romance novel.

Having read no more than a couple of pages, she felt her head falling forward, her eyes starting to close. Waking with a start when she heard the front door of the house slam closed, she realised it was over an hour later.

'Martin, is that you?' she called, still only half awake. 'Martin, I'm in my living room,' she called again, hearing a knock on her apartment door.

'Hey, Grams,' said Martin, kissing her on the cheek before he slumped his lanky body down into the armchair opposite her. 'How's the court case going?'

'You know I can't tell you that.'

'It was all over the news today. Even the Prime Minister—'

'Stop right there, Martin Roscoe. You know I can't talk about it.'

'But do you think he's guilty?'

'Stop it, before I get annoyed.'

'Okay – whatever,' said Martin, pretending to sulk.

'Tell me what's been going on with you?' said Jessie.

'Not much. School. Track. Same.'

'Nothing else?'

'Not really.'

'You know you can talk to me whenever you want, Martin.'

''Bout what?'

'That's the thing, Martin, I don't know,' said Jessie, desperately trying not to show her frustration. 'Perhaps you should tell me?'

'There's nothing to tell, Grams. Just the same old shit.'

Telling herself to ignore Martin's language, Jessie could see something was wrong. No grandmother could be prouder of her grandson than she was – an A-student in class, a national track champion but, like all kids, he looked for the chance to push boundaries whenever he could. Jessie knew that and it didn't worry her. What did worry her was Martin going missing and not telling his father where he had been.

'Your dad knows you missed school yesterday,' said Jessie.

Martin rolled his eyes and put his feet up on her coffee table. She raised her eyebrows in a manner she felt Judge Phillips would have been proud of, and Martin quickly took his feet down.

'And what about the track meet?' added Jessie. 'You never miss track.'

Martin folded his arms across his chest.

'Who told him I missed track?' he asked angrily.

'Don't you raise your voice at me, Martin Roscoe.'

'I bet it was George. That's the last time I trust him.'

'So you did miss track?'

'Hey, enough with your questions, Grams,' said Martin, springing to his feet. 'You're not in court now.'

'Martin!' shouted Jessie, as her grandson stormed from the room, slamming the door behind him.

'And I think the Prime Minister's guilty,' he shouted as he ran out of the apartment and up the stairs into the rest of the house he shared with his father.

Jessie rested her head in her hands. Martin wasn't the kind of boy to behave in this way. Something was wrong; she just wished she knew what it was.

CHAPTER 15

ROSCOE WALKED BRISKLY THROUGH the hotel and out into the employee parking lot at the rear.

He checked his watch. The Prime Minister would be arriving in less than three minutes.

The call had come directly from the Downing Street private office, and Roscoe had immediately put the hotel's VIP protocol into place. Rapid passage was to be given to Andrew Turner through the hotel and up to the fourteenth floor. This was a private visit and was to be treated on a strictly confidential, need-to-know basis.

As he stood at the employee entrance, Roscoe received a call from Stanley, who was working the arrival with him.

'Boss, he's here,' said Stanley. 'He's pulling round to the rear of the hotel now. Black Jaguar. From what I can make out, the VIP is the driver and he is travelling alone.'

'Alone?' replied Roscoe, surprised. He'd never heard of a British Prime Minister, past or present, travelling without some security entourage.

'Can confirm, Boss. He's pulling up to the rear-entrance barrier now. VIP is driving and it looks like he's alone.'

At the far end of the garage Stanley raised the security barrier, and Roscoe watched the black-windowed car slowly enter. With Stanley walking behind, the car edged its way down the aisle, before turning into a reserved bay as indicated by Roscoe. As the engine was extinguished, the lights on the vehicle went dark, but the car's driver remained inside.

By now, Stanley was standing beside Roscoe and turned to his boss.

'I could definitely see the PM driving. Tough to see if anyone else was in the rear, but can't imagine there would be,' he said.

'It is just him,' replied Roscoe.

'How long do we wait?'

'Guess he's got a lot on his mind,' Roscoe smiled.

At that moment the driver's door started to open and Roscoe walked forward to the vehicle, offering his hand to the Prime Minister. But as Andrew Turner stepped from the car, an explosion of light burst through the parking lot.

A high-powered photo lens was rapidly taking pictures from across the garage.

Spotting the photographer in the shadows, Roscoe instructed Stanley to take the Prime Minister to the employee elevator, as he stormed across the parking lot in pursuit of the man. While Stanley scooped his bear-like arm around Turner and walked him quickly inside the hotel, Roscoe ran across the tops of three cars, before jumping down only feet from the man who was dressed head-to-toe in black, with a beanie hat pulled down over his head. Realising Roscoe was in close pursuit, the man scrambled around a giant Tribeca Hotels SUV, his camera catching on the wing-mirror and crashing to the ground as he did.

Roscoe watched as the man ran, abandoning his kit as he made his way out of the rear of the garage. Picking up the camera, Roscoe knew he had what he needed. He gave up the chase and quickly made his way back inside the hotel.

'Apologies, Prime Minister,' said Roscoe, holding up the camera as he approached Turner and Stanley, 'but no damage done. I will make sure all the images are deleted.'

'I would be most grateful,' replied Turner. 'And thank you both for your discretion in such a difficult matter.'

'We pride ourselves on the utmost discretion at Tribeca Hotels, Prime Minister, you can be assured of that,' said Roscoe, as he accompanied Turner into the elevator. As they travelled through the building, Roscoe looked at the man who held such power. Standing next to him, he seemed so vulnerable. Roscoe knew it was his job to provide the security and diplomacy for which Tribeca Luxury

Hotels was so renowned, but he did wonder if he was giving assistance to a man who truly warranted such attention.

As the elevator doors opened and the Prime Minister briefly shook Roscoe's hand, he wondered what exactly Turner's role in the Elegant Daniels affair had been. He watched him walk down the hallway to the Rylands' suite, where the door was already open.

Was Roscoe looking at a man already making his final walk towards the political gallows?

CHAPTER 16

HUMILIATION WAS A FEELING to which Amelia Rylands was becoming immune.

Lying on her bed, she turned the pages of *The London Informer* and even though she had spent the day in the Old Bailey, she found it almost impossible to comprehend what she was reading. The paper had run a splash front-page headline, 'PM EYES HARVEY'S GIRL', accompanied by page upon page of photographs of Elegant Daniels standing on the courthouse steps.

Inside the paper, Amelia read a profile of herself, asking how she could survive each day, as she sat in court, exposed to the actions of her cheating husband. 'Still maintaining her dignity somehow, Amelia Rylands appears each day in support of her husband – a husband who, for twenty years, has chased after women the world over, without a second thought for his loyal wife.'

As Amelia read and reread the story, she heard the Prime Minister enter the living room of their private suite.

'I don't have long,' said Andrew Turner, demonstrating the force of personality that had led him to the highest office in the land. 'I'm taking a huge risk in coming here, but what the hell is your counsel doing, introducing me into this case? And don't tell me they didn't lead her into it, because I've read the transcript.'

'Good evening, Prime Minister,' replied Rylands. Amelia recognised the familiar sound of her husband dropping ice cubes into a tumbler as he poured himself another glass of single-malt whisky. 'I have absolutely no idea what you mean.'

'Don't know what I mean?' said Turner, and Amelia heard him cross the room towards her husband. 'And you don't need any more of this,' he went on, as Amelia imagined him removing the glass from Harvey's grasp. 'You used me as nothing more than a diversionary tactic,' continued the Prime Minister. Amelia was able to hear the anger surfacing in his tone. 'How dare you? And after everything my family has done for you; the times I've bailed you out of one mess or another. How dare you!' he exclaimed. 'You've simply no idea the political pressure I'm coming under.'

'Andrew, calm down,' Rylands said, as the sound of him preparing himself another drink reached Amelia's bedroom. 'If anyone should be getting stressed right now, it should be me.'

'Don't tell me to calm down, Harvey,' said Turner, to the sound of his fist hitting one of the antique leather Chesterfield armchairs that furnished the room. 'Can you imagine what Barbara would have made of this?' he continued. 'You're dragging me through the mud all over again. It's all you ever do! Look, nobody wants you to be acquitted more than I do . . .'

'I'm not sure that's entirely true, Andrew,' said Rylands.

'You know what I mean. I can't have my ex-brother-in-law languishing somewhere at Her Majesty's pleasure. For Christ's sake, Harvey, I've made a pledge to cut the prison population – not have my family add to it.'

'I really don't know what you're expecting me to say, Prime Minister. Your name came up in court today – simple as that.'

'But your counsel led her there.'

'In evidence, Andrew,' said Rylands, with a patronising calm. 'She was under oath, what else could she say?'

'You're using me,' said Turner, sounding exasperated. 'Look, Harvey, you need to know this. I'm talking to the Attorney General. I'm thinking of putting a statement out in the morning.'

'You can't comment on an ongoing case!' said Rylands, his own anger suddenly surfacing.

'Don't you try and lecture me on the law. We will do everything possible to avoid prejudice, but I have to defend my position.'

Amelia could hear both men speaking in increasingly angry voices.

'This isn't just about me and my marriage,' continued Turner. 'This is about the party and the government. You need to understand that the government could fall, as a result of your trial.'

'And I could end up being put away!'

Amelia got to her feet and began to edge slowly towards her bedroom door. As she did so, she heard Andrew Turner pour himself a drink from the decanter, then the creak of leather told her he had seated himself beside her husband.

'Harvey, we both know there is not – and never has been – any question of a relationship between me and this woman Elegant Daniels, don't we?' asserted the Prime Minister.

There was silence and Amelia waited for her husband. After a long pause he replied.

'If I take the stand tomorrow,' Rylands began slowly, 'and attest to the fact that you never had a relationship with her, it will leave me as the only realistic suspect for the jury to consider. Why would I do that?'

'I don't care why, Harvey. If you don't do it, I will. I'm not being set up as an alternative suspect in your attempted-murder trial!'

'You don't get it, Andrew,' said Rylands, speaking in a low voice. 'I'm going to take the stand and I'm going to say whatever it takes. The only thing that will stop me is you starting to pull some very big strings. I'm looking at a lot worse than losing my job, or being a threat to your party. I'm looking at twenty years. I will say whatever it takes to create a reasonable doubt.'

'Harvey, you have to be realistic here,' said Turner, as Amelia thought he sounded increasingly defensive. 'I just don't have that kind of influence. I have to let the judiciary run its own course.'

'Andrew,' smiled Rylands, speaking slowly, 'I'm on trial for attempted murder, and I'm staying in the world's most luxurious hotel chain. This doesn't happen to normal defendants, and I know it wasn't just my money that has secured me this little privilege.'

'Pre-trial is one thing, but I can't interfere with a verdict.'

Amelia heard her husband get to his feet and return to the bar.

'Can't or won't? Come on, Andrew, we all know how it works. A couple of calls from you lead to a couple more calls and, before we know it, there is a bit of pressure on the judge. A statement from him pushing the jury in my direction – that's all I'm asking. And if that doesn't work, there are always the appeal judges.'

'No, Harvey, you're on your own this time. Neither my influence nor Barbara's money is going to get you out of this.'

'Don't throw Barbara's money at me! What got you into Downing Street in the first place?'

Rylands took another long drink. 'We both know any statement from you denying a relationship with Elegant would be a downright lie. And if you don't help me, I will take the stand tomorrow and tell the world exactly what did happen between the two of you.'

CHAPTER 17

LISTENING INTENTLY, AMELIA PULLED her robe tightly around her slender waist. As she stood by the door she could hear her husband's threatening tone.

'The only reason you've come here tonight is to find out what I might say on the stand; to try and bully me into putting you in the clear; to make sure good ol' Harvey will play ball. Well, Andrew, I won't, not this time. I'm fighting for my life – and if you don't help me, I will do whatever it takes.'

'Harvey, you've got this all wrong,' said Turner, a calming tone in his voice. 'We're all in this together.'

Amelia smiled to herself, hearing a statement that couldn't be further from the truth.

'Andrew, you introduced me to her.'

'I may have done in passing. I don't recall.'

'For crying out loud, you're not at Prime Minister's Questions now. You don't recall – don't be ridiculous,' said

Rylands, and Amelia could hear the increasingly aggressive edge in his voice. 'Don't bullshit me.'

She crept forward until, standing in the drawing-room doorway, she could see the rage in both men's eyes.

'I know everything,' Rylands continued. 'The secrets you shared with her, the promises you made, the fact that you were fucking her long before I ever met her.' Amelia watched Harvey move towards Andrew Turner, stopping only inches from his face. 'And that you're still fucking her, even now. I bet that's a real turn-on. Maybe you should put that in your statement.'

'Don't be ridiculous. How can you know that?'

'I might not be Prime Minister, but I do have people who tell me things.'

'You're in no position to be making threats, Harvey.'

'I'm in every position. I could be sent down tomorrow. I know the promises you made.'

'For God's sake, Harvey, I was moving into Downing Street with my wife. What the hell did you think I was going to do? Move her in next door at Number Eleven? Anyway, what do you care? I passed her on to you, didn't I?'

Amelia saw the fierce passion in Harvey's eyes.

'This mess is of your making!' Turner shouted. 'I'm not getting you out of this one. I'm issuing the statement.'

Fearing what Harvey might do next, Amelia stepped into the room.

'Andrew, good evening,' she said, wanting to radiate calm.

'Amelia, hello,' said the Prime Minister, clearly surprised by her entrance. 'I didn't realise you were here. May I say that, despite everything, somehow you still manage to look amazing.'

'Thank you,' said Amelia, turning her cheek to the Prime Minister as he crossed the room to greet her. 'Each day gets harder and harder,' she continued, 'but right now, I couldn't care less what you or Harvey did with that woman. What I do care about is what happens next – to all of us. Threatening each other will get us nowhere.'

She walked across the room and poured herself a glass of whisky, before sitting on the arm of one of the leather chairs.

'Andrew, we understand this puts you in a horrendous position, but we have to deal with where we are. We're getting near the end of the trial. We don't expect any favours, but what we do ask is for you not to damage us. Wait until the verdict, and then begin your fight-back. We have to believe the evidence will deliver us the result we all want.'

Amelia looked at her husband as he took another long drink from his glass.

'We can ride this out. Harvey hasn't set out to damage you, but we have to do everything we can to get the outcome we need in court. Once the trial is over and we have the right verdict, we can all move forward.'

The room fell into silence.

The two men looked at Amelia and then at each other. Leaning forward, she smiled.

'Destroying each other is not the way out of this.'

CHAPTER 18

A PHOTOGRAPHER'S CAMERA SLAMMED against the back window of the high-powered Tribeca Hotel's SUV, as early the next morning Roscoe edged the car forward through the crowd of media and onlookers stationed outside the Old Bailey. A flash burst into life, illuminating the inside of the car as another camera lens crashed against the window.

Looking in his rear-view mirror, Roscoe saw both Harvey Rylands and his wife flinch, turning momentarily towards each other. Inside the car Roscoe knew they were safe; outside the car, they would be on their own.

Watching the couple during the journey from the hotel, he had sensed a growing tension between them. Each day of the trial had seen them appear together, but as the evidence was placed before the court, it seemed to him that it was becoming harder and harder for Mrs Rylands to remain the loyal wife, standing so valiantly by her man.

Looking at her now, he saw a woman who was exhausted. It was two weeks since the Rylands had arrived at Tribeca;

each day Amelia had lost more and more of her vitality. Even her shiny blonde hair had somehow lost its sheen.

The requirement each day was for her to step from the car and portray her marriage as a happy one. How did she do it? Guilty or not, her husband had cheated on her remorselessly, without the slightest regard for her feelings.

The media scrum outside the courthouse had reached an unprecedented level; what Roscoe saw could only be described as a frenzy. Questions about the Prime Minister's relationship with Elegant Daniels were hurled at the car; fists were slammed onto its roof. His passengers were both hidden inside their own space; each so distant, each paying scant regard to the other.

Until the vehicle stopped. And they stepped out onto the courthouse steps.

Harvey Rylands emerged, with his wife tightly clutching his arm – both of them vulnerable and, to all appearances, still desperately in love. Amelia Rylands once again standing loyally at her husband's side, as they forged a path through the chaos and into the building.

CHAPTER 19

BEFORE THE FINAL WITNESS for the defence was called, fatigue had briefly threatened to overwhelm Jessie Luck, as the trial drew on and she sat in the jury box gently massaging her knee. But as soon as Harvey Rylands was led from the dock and onto the stand, a bolt of electricity shot through the courtroom and Jessie joined everyone present in anticipating his evidence. She listened as he raised his right hand, swearing the oath, and she thought how condescending he sounded, for a man who needed to deliver the most convincing performance of his life.

Humphrey Adams, QC, began his questioning by asking his client about his relationship with Elegant Daniels.

'I cared for her deeply,' said Rylands. 'I think I probably still do. I've known her for over a year, and we have been intimate for much of that. I loved her. In my heart, I believe we loved each other.'

'It has been suggested, Mr Rylands, that on the night of the attack upon Ms Daniels you had argued over your future?'

'There is no point in me denying I have a temper; my wife could most certainly attest to that. But I have never been a violent man, and I am sure she would equally attest to that.'

Jessie looked across at Amelia Rylands, who simply dropped her head, avoiding any eye contact with the court.

'Ms Daniels and I did argue on the night of the attack. I wish we hadn't – perhaps somehow it would have made things different – but we did. Elegant wanted to speak of our future, but while I loved her, I have a wife to whom I have been married for over twenty years, and this is not something to be thrown away lightly – if, in my mind, at all.'

Jessie eased back in her chair. In her view, she didn't hear a husband desperately in love, but one trapped in an obligation to maintain his marriage. Rylands continued his evidence, talking through his relationship with Ms Daniels: how he was happy to assist in supporting her financially; how they had enjoyed dinner together earlier in the evening on the night of the attack; and how he left her home shortly after 1 a.m.

'You drove away from the parking lot, Mr Rylands?'

'Yes.'

'And where did you go?'

'I headed straight home. It's about a fifteen-minute drive.'

'And how did you feel at this point?'

'I felt annoyed that we'd argued; frustrated about my relationship with Elegant. I needed to talk it through with someone.'

'Indeed?' said Mr Adams. 'And did you have anyone you were able to talk to?'

'I did,' said Rylands, pausing.

'Go on, Mr Rylands?'

'I made a telephone call.'

Lifting his spectacles, Humphrey Adams looked inquisitively at his client and waited for him to continue.

'I called my brother-in-law. Andrew Turner, the Prime Minister.'

CHAPTER 20

RELIEVED TO LEAVE THE chaos of the courthouse behind him, Roscoe drove back through the busy central London streets, before pulling into the employee parking lot at the Tribeca Luxury Hotel. Turning into his reserved bay, he was surprised to see Maggie Owen, one of the hotel's chambermaids, come running towards him.

Instantly Roscoe could see that she was frantic.

Waving her arms and gasping for air as she desperately tried to hold back her tears, she screamed at Roscoe to stop the car. Coming to an immediate stop and jumping from the vehicle, he saw make-up-stained tears streaking down her face.

'Maggie, take a breath and tell me what's wrong,' he said.

'You have to help,' she cried desperately, rubbing the tears from her face, smearing her eye make-up even more as she did so.

'What's happened?' Roscoe took hold of her hand and she started to lead him towards the hotel. 'Stand still and tell me what's going on.'

'It's Lily. She's gone.'

Lily was Maggie's seven-year-old daughter. Roscoe had met her at the barbecue that the hotel hosted for all its employees and their families, the week before the grand opening. With her long black hair tied back in pink ribbons, Lily had reminded him of his own twin daughters.

'I want you to tell me exactly what's happened,' he instructed, putting his arm around Maggie while walking her back to the employee entrance.

'It's all my fault,' she sobbed. 'Lily said she didn't feel well this morning, and I didn't want to take a day off work and she did have a bit of a temperature, so I said she could stay off school. But I said she had to come with me and sit in one of the staff lounges and practise her reading. I should have made her go to school – I know I should've. I was so stupid.'

'Don't worry, Maggie, we'll find her,' said Roscoe, thinking the child couldn't have gone far. 'So, you left her downstairs?'

'Yes, you know what it's like – there are people coming and going all the time in the main lounge. I said I would check back every half hour to see how she was doing.'

'So when did you last go back and check?'

'It must be twenty minutes ago. I thought I'd take her upstairs with me for a while. But she's gone, Jon, gone!'

Seeing the look of desperation on Maggie's face, Roscoe knew exactly how she felt.

'Let's get downstairs and I'll get a full search started. Have you spoken to Stanley?'

'No, I've been looking on my own.'

'Let me call him and he can head up the physical search. You know how impossible it is to get anywhere inside the hotel without the proper access.'

Maggie stopped and turned. 'I've done something stupid. I gave Lily my pass,' she said, before continuing quickly, 'I know I shouldn't have and I know it's against the rules, but I thought it would be easier. She could go to the bathroom if she needed to, and if she wanted to see me, she could just get into the elevator. That's why I went back down. I needed my pass. God help me, what have I done?'

Roscoe knew Maggie had acted only with the best intentions, but in that moment the search for Lily had become far more complicated. Now was not the time to be concerned with breaches in security, though, and as he headed inside, Roscoe called Stanley and instructed him to put in place a floor-by-floor search of all public areas of the hotel. With Maggie's pass, Lily could access any one of the hotel's forty floors, as well as the rooms her mum had been assigned that day.

Leading Maggie into the hotel's security control room, he explained that the best place for them to start was with the recorded security images from the past forty minutes.

'If we can spot where Lily headed when she left the staff lounge, we'll have her found in no time,' he reassured her. 'She won't have gone far, Maggie, I'm sure.'

With her sitting beside him in front of the security screens, Roscoe could feel Maggie holding her breath as he rolled back the images of the hallway outside the staff lounge. While the camera didn't give a clear picture of the room itself, it did show the hallway leading away from the room.

At first there was nothing but the empty hall.

And then Maggie let out an agonising cry.

Viewed from behind, walking down the hallway, her Queen Elsa backpack almost bigger than her, was Lily.

Hand-in-hand with an unknown man.

CHAPTER 21

SITTING IN THE OLD Bailey jury box, Jessie Luck listened attentively as the judge issued his final instructions to the jury. Humphrey Adams had completed his questioning of Harvey Rylands by entering into evidence the phone log from Rylands' mobile phone, showing that a call had been made at 1.19 a.m. on the morning of the attack, to the Prime Minister's private line in Downing Street. The call had lasted a little over four minutes, and Rylands claimed the conversation with his brother-in-law, whom he regarded as a close friend, was to tell him how he'd argued with Elegant, leaving him at a loss as to the way forward in their relationship.

What happened after that call? wondered Jessie.

Humphrey Adams had pressed Rylands further on his friendship with the Prime Minister. It was a relationship that had lasted for more than thirty years, Rylands said, and had survived the death of the Prime Minister's older half-sister, Barbara, his first wife. Upon her death, Rylands confirmed that he had inherited great wealth, through her business. Asked to speculate on the rubies that had become such a symbol in the case, Rylands said he believed they might have come from one of the mines he inherited at the time of his wife's passing. The judge intervened when Adams asked Rylands how he believed the Prime Minister would have felt about Harvey inheriting such great wealth from Barbara, but in her mind Jessie had already answered that question.

As the judge spoke directly to the jury, he stressed the need to consider only the direct evidence they had heard in his courtroom. They must not speculate on the actions of others not called to testify, or any actions not offered in evidence in the court. Any prior knowledge of the case, the people involved or information garnered from press reports or media speculation before they undertook their role as jurors, must also be disregarded. And he emphatically told them that any press coverage they had seen during the case must in no way influence the decision they were about to reach.

Walking in silence with her fellow jurors, down the hallway at the rear of the court towards the jury room, Jessie felt the weight of the case sitting heavily on her. Arguments put forward by the defence had suggested other possible suspects for the attack. Elegant Daniels had had relationships with many other men, including the Prime Minister, who was intrinsically linked to the case; yet evidence had demonstrated that

Harvey Rylands had been in her room on the night of the attack. Jessie was also aware that the video showing his car's later return to the parking lot was unclear, but if it hadn't been Rylands in the car, why had Elegant Daniels been so certain he was the man attacking her?

The first decision Jessie was faced with, as she took her seat at the table, was who to support in the role of foreperson. For her, this was the easiest decision of the week. The city banker nominating himself had not spoken more than three words to her throughout the trial; the retired head teacher had sat and eaten sandwiches with her most days during the lunch break, and Jessie was reassured when she was easily elected to lead them in their deliberations.

To give clarity to their immediate position, it was decided to cast an initial confidential ballot of the jurors.

Marking her paper, Jessie carried her burden of responsibility heavily. She was being asked to exercise her judgment on Harvey Rylands, and decide whether he was guilty or not guilty.

In her mind, there was only one answer.

CHAPTER 22

ROSCOE FELT HIS STOMACH tighten as he looked at the screen and watched Lily walking away from him, down the hallway.

'We've got to go after them,' said Maggie, getting to her feet, ready to race out into the hall.

'Wait,' said Roscoe, reaching up a hand to Maggie, the calmness of his voice not betraying the rising concern he felt. 'This video is from more than twenty minutes ago. We need to watch where they go.'

He clicked the image forward to the next camera.

The pair walked hand-in-hand down the hall, Lily still skipping beside the unknown man.

Maggie stood frozen.

'I've told her so many times, Jon. Never, never go anywhere with a stranger.' She began to weep again and, moving to the next image, Roscoe could offer her no comfort.

Seeing the image change, Maggie dropped back into her chair, crying out as she stared at the screen.

'He's taking her to the elevators.'

Roscoe reached across to Maggie, who was now looking at the video through open fingers, her hands clasped to her face.

Still holding Lily's hand, the man stepped forward and pressed the elevator call button.

Within seconds the elevator arrived.

The doors opened.

Dragging her backpack behind her, Lily stepped inside.

Followed by the unidentified man.

The doors closed.

And they were gone.

'Where's he taken her?' Maggie screamed. 'Where is she?'

Roscoe held the image on the closed elevator door, then rolled it backwards. He watched again as the man walked hand-in-hand with Lily down the hallway, before hitting the elevator call button.

There was something familiar about him.

Roscoe watched the image again.

Who was this man?

Again the elevator doors opened.

Again Lily stepped inside.

Followed by the man.

Once again, Roscoe rolled back the image.

And then moved it forward, frame by frame, until he could see inside the elevator.

Staring back at Roscoe, from the immaculately polished mirror at the back of the elevator, was a face he knew.

The South African-born journalist determined to trespass upon Tribeca property.

Michael Madison.

CHAPTER 23

BURNING WITH ANGER, ROSCOE sprinted down the hallway of the fourteenth floor. Michael Madison was standing motionless in the doorway of the Rylands' suite – a frightened deer in sight of an oncoming ten-ton truck.

Immobile, he simply said, 'I can explain.'

Roscoe saw his mouth move, but didn't hear a word.

Without a break in his momentum, he launched all of his six-foot three-inch, two-hundred-pound frame forward in a single motion, landing a right hook squarely on Madison's jaw. With not a split second to react, Madison was felled with the single shot and crumpled unconscious on the floor.

As soon as he had seen Madison's image in the elevator mirror, Roscoe had known where he had taken Lily. Quickly he led Maggie to the elevator bank and, while riding up to the fourteenth floor, reassured her that the unscrupulous journalist's only interest in taking Lily was to secure himself unfettered access to the Rylands' suite.

'Don't cry, Mummy,' said Lily, as her mother ran down the hallway towards her. 'Don't be sad,' she said as she walked out of the suite, still carrying her oversized backpack, before being swept up in Maggie's arms.

'Oh, Lily, I'm not sad. I'm happy, so very, very happy,' said Maggie, hugging her child so tightly Roscoe thought she would never let her go.

'All okay?' asked Roscoe, quietly.

Wiping tears from her eyes, Maggie looked up at him.

'Thank you so much, Jon. I thought I was never going to see her again.'

Roscoe shared in Maggie's joy and, as she picked up her daughter, he couldn't help but wrap his arms around them both, before Maggie carried Lily down the hall. As they walked away, the elevator doors opened and Roscoe saw Stanley coming towards him.

'A gentleman of the press for you to deal with,' said Roscoe to his assistant, gesturing towards Madison, who had regained consciousness, but remained slumped against the heavy wooden door that led into the suite, 'although I have to say he's anything but a gentleman.'

Roscoe stepped back over to the journalist, stood directly over him and, resting his boot on Madison's hand, let his full body weight crush the journalist's fingers.

Madison cried for mercy.

'I'm sorry, Roscoe!' he begged. 'I didn't do anything to hurt her.'

Roscoe twisted his boot, before releasing the pressure.

'You stupid little rat. I should have drowned you when I had the chance.'

'I needed to get into the suite, and you were never going to help me.'

'Help you!' exclaimed Roscoe, towering over Madison.

'I was desperate. If anyone stopped me, I was simply taking her to see her mum.'

Incredulous, Roscoe shook his head.

'You kidnapped a seven-year-old girl. I should have you locked up.'

'I never meant her any harm. To be honest, I couldn't believe my luck.'

'Luck?' said Roscoe. 'You call it luck? I call it absolute stupidity.'

Still ablaze with anger, he jumped forward onto Madison's outstretched knee, crushing the joint. As Madison hollered in pain, Roscoe stepped back and turned away.

'Take him away, Stanley, before I do something I'll really regret.'

'He's not worth it, Boss,' said Stanley, grabbing the journalist by the jacket collar and hauling him to his feet.

Roscoe thought of Maggie holding her daughter so tightly to her, the most precious thing in the world. He couldn't stop himself. He turned again, grabbed Madison by the throat and slammed him into the wall.

'You are total scum. Aren't you?' he shouted, his face pressing into the journalist's. 'You'd better swear never to do anything as fucking stupid again.'

'Never! Never ever,' pleaded Madison.

'Get this filth out of my sight,' said Roscoe, releasing him and letting Stanley march the journalist down the hall and into the waiting elevator.

Walking behind them, Roscoe took a deep breath.

Further down the hall he stopped and crouched down to talk to Lily, as she held tightly onto her mother.

'Hello, Lily,' he said softly, 'my name's Jon.'

'Hello,' replied a tiny voice.

'Do you think you might be able to help me?' asked Roscoe.

Clinging to her mother, her fists tightly balled, Lily nodded her head.

'Can you tell me what the man was doing inside the big room?'

'I don't know,' said Lily.

'Do you think he was playing hide-and-seek?' smiled Roscoe.

'No,' Lily laughed. 'He wasn't playing,' she said. 'He was looking for something.'

'And did he find anything?'

'I don't think so. He was in a hurry.'

'I bet he was. Do you know what room he was looking in?'

'In the bedrooms. He went inside the people's bags,' Lily told Roscoe. 'He shouldn't have done that, should he? They weren't his bags.'

'You're right, he shouldn't.'

'I told him, but he said it was okay. I didn't believe him. He was being naughty, wasn't he? That's why you hit him.'

Roscoe looked up at Maggie.

'Perhaps I shouldn't have hit him quite so hard,' said Roscoe, 'but he was being very naughty.'

Lily nodded her head and smiled.

'And when he was looking in the people's bags, where did you go, Lily?'

Lily dropped her head and curled into her mother.

'It's okay,' said Maggie, 'you can tell Jon. You won't get into trouble.'

Having seen the scarlet lipstick smudged on her face, Roscoe could guess how Lily had entertained herself.

'Did you go into the lady's make-up bag?' he asked.

Lily nodded her head.

'I was looking for Mummy and then, when I couldn't find her, he said I should look after myself.'

'I'm sure the lady won't mind, but we'll keep it as our secret, if you like. You, me and Mummy. '

Lily nodded.

'Good,' said Roscoe, standing back up to his full height and rubbing Lily's hair affectionately as he did so. 'Can I ask you one more thing?' He crouched back down. 'What are you keeping so safe in your hands?'

Lily stared at Roscoe.

'We'll make it our secret as well,' said Roscoe. 'I promise.'

'Like the lipstick?' asked Lily.

'Yes, like the lipstick,' reassured Roscoe. 'Our secret.'

Slowly Lily put her hands out in front of her, unfurling her little fingers as she did so.

Clenched in the palm of each was a dazzling, blood-red ruby.

CHAPTER 24

ROSCOE LOOKED UP AT Maggie, who gasped in pure amazement at the stunning rubies her daughter was holding. Aware that Maggie was about to start to quiz Lily on where the jewels had come from, he gently held up his hand.

'Wow, look at those jewels!' he said to Lily. 'They're amazing. And such a shiny red. Can I hold one?'

With some reluctance Lily reached across, releasing one of her treasures to Roscoe.

'Thank you,' he said, smiling at Lily. 'It's very beautiful, isn't it?'

Lily nodded her head.

'Can you tell me where you found them?'

Lily looked at Roscoe and bit her lip. She turned to look at her mother, who leaned down beside her.

'It's okay, Lily. You can tell Jon where you found the jewels. We won't be angry.'

Lily was silent.

'Let me guess. Did you find them in the kitchen?' smiled Roscoe.

Lily shook her head.

'Did you find them in the living room?'

Again, she shook her head.

'Was it the dining room?'

'No, silly!' Lily laughed. 'It was in the bathroom.'

'In the man's bathroom?' asked Roscoe.

Lily frowned, shaking her head.

'The lady's?' said Roscoe, a questioning rise in his voice.

Roscoe watched Lily nod her head, almost as if she was amazed it had taken Roscoe so long to guess.

'In with her make-up?' he asked.

'Yes!' exclaimed Lily.

'Why don't you give Jon the other jewel, so he can take them back to the lady's room?' said Maggie. Lily grudgingly handed the jewel over to Roscoe, giving him a hug as she did so.

'Promise me you won't go wandering off without your mum again,' said Roscoe, getting to his feet and heading down the hallway.

'Thanks for everything, Jon,' called Maggie, but Roscoe was already approaching the door to the Rylands' suite.

Why rubies? he thought. He knew the shocking part they had played in the Elegant Daniels attack, but why were there more rubies in the Rylands' suite? Why bring more rubies to the hotel? What did they mean?

With Tribeca Luxury Hotels' commitment to guest space being sacrosanct ringing in his ears, as he entered the bathroom, Roscoe couldn't stop his detective's instinct kicking in. Picking up the vanity case, he started to search through its contents. Taking out the first layer, he found nothing out of the ordinary. A second layer of cosmetics with a pocket for the rubies followed; but then, taking out the third, he found a clear plastic wallet concealed at the bottom of the case.

Removing the wallet, he discovered a set of papers and, upon opening them, realised they were legal documents, dated a number of years earlier.

Paging through the papers, Roscoe understood what he was holding.

Divorce papers for Barbara Turner and Harvey Rylands.

CHAPTER 25

FOLDING THE PAPERS AND slipping them into his back pocket, Roscoe returned the layers of the vanity case, before heading out of the room. Taking the elevator down to the security control room, he recollected the death of Barbara Turner from more than twenty years before. At the time her half-brother, Andrew, was a relatively unknown junior government minister, and her death had been widely reported, due to her own notoriety rather than his.

Barbara Turner had been one of the most influential figures in British industry, owning mining and manufacturing assets across the globe – her achievements all the more notable in that they came through a company originally established by her mother immediately after the Second World War.

Portrayed by the press as a ball-breaker, Barbara had a reputation that was ill-deserved, and which Roscoe knew was constructed by a media trying to fill the gap generated by her desire to protect her privacy. Her marriage was always viewed as turbulent, but Roscoe thought any marriage to Harvey Rylands would be a tempestuous one.

Trying to remember more details, Roscoe logged into the Tribeca Luxury Hotels global communication network, and seconds later Josh Jameson, Head of Security for the three Australian Tribeca Hotels, appeared on the screen in front of him.

'Hey, Roscoe, what's going on?' came the Australian's greeting. 'I was about to head out for dinner.'

'Sorry for disturbing your evening,' replied Roscoe, knowing full well that the head of his team in the southern hemisphere never let himself be off-duty, even when he was off climbing mountains. 'I need some help on an old case.'

'Fire away,' said the ever-helpful Aussie, the youngest member of Roscoe's global team. 'What do you need?'

'Do you remember the death of the British businesswoman Barbara Turner?'

'Remember it? I think I was about seven at the time,' laughed Jameson, 'but I know the case. She was the woman who went overboard from her yacht, sailing round the Barrier Reef?'

'That's the one,' said Roscoe, the details of the case coming back to him.

'Middle of the night, everyone said she was drunk, stumbled out of her cabin, fell over the side of the boat and drowned. Sad story. She was a wealthy woman, right?'

'Very.'

'And now her husband is up for attempted murder, that's right?'

'You know about the Rylands case?'

'Chief, we might be the other side of the world, but we do still get news stories! Why are you interested?'

'I'm not sure,' said Roscoe. 'Rylands is staying here at the hotel, along with his current wife. There could be a verdict today, but there are a couple of things that don't quite add up and I'm wondering if somehow they link back to Barbara. Can you get me some more details on the case?'

'I know how you hate loose ends. What are you looking for?'

'Passenger lists, anything from the autopsy on Barbara Turner, something in the police records not made public.'

'Leave it with me. I'll make a couple of calls, see what I can find.'

'Josh, you said you were seven at the time?'

'Something like that,' said Jameson, clicking on his keyboard. 'Six in fact, Chief. *Sydney Morning Herald* reports the accident as happening on November the twenty-second 1995.'

'You're sickeningly young,' laughed Roscoe. 'Can I leave this with you?'

'No problem. Call you back in thirty,' said Jameson, disconnecting the line.

Roscoe leaned back in his chair, pulling the Barbara Turner–Harvey Rylands divorce papers from his pocket as he did so.

Reading through them again, something immediately struck him.

They were dated November 22nd 1995.

CHAPTER 26

SITTING ALONE AND IN silence, with the Old Bailey courtroom once again filling around her, Amelia Rylands felt an equal sense of expectation and dread. All her hopes rested upon the verdict that the jury in her husband's trial for attempted murder was about to deliver.

She looked across at the twelve-person jury as they filed back in and took their seats across from the judge's bench. Desperate for some kind of sign, she quickly tried to catch the eye of the older black woman who had smiled reassuringly towards her on more than one occasion during the trial.

For the briefest moment she caught her eye.

But the woman turned quickly away.

Thoughts raced around Amelia's head. Why didn't the woman want to look at her? Dropping her head, she inhaled deeply as she clasped her hands tightly together.

Clasped in prayer.

For Harvey.

Clasped so tightly that, as the Clerk of the Court collected the verdict from the jury foreperson, her fingernails cut into her soft skin.

A narrow line of blood ran down the back of her hand. Transfixed, as the verdict was handed to the judge, Amelia never noticed.

As he considered the jury's decision in silence, her prayers continued. Holding her breath, both hands bloodied now, she watched the judge return the verdict to the clerk.

She touched her fingers to her face, tasting blood on her lips, as the clerk read the verdict aloud.

Guilty.

CHAPTER 27

SEATED IN FRONT OF the main monitor in the hotel's security control room, Roscoe saw the call request come in from Josh Jameson and instantly hit the Accept key.

'Josh, what have you got for me?' asked Roscoe.

'Hey, Chief, look, I've spoken to an old contact at New South Wales Police and they've made some calls north for me. From what I can make out, most things are pretty much as reported in the press at the time. A beautiful summer's evening, waters were real still, but somehow in the middle of the night Barbara Turner ends up overboard. She and Harvey had been out on the water all day, and seemingly both spent pretty much most of that time drinking. The record shows a call was made to the coastguard soon after five in the morning, and at that point a full search-and-rescue operation was put into place, but it was too late.'

'And who made that call?'

'Captain of the boat, on the instruction of Harvey Rylands.'

'But definitely no call until five a.m.?'

'No, and the overall timeline is a little bit shaky. Rylands reported they'd both been drinking until past two in the morning. Crew on board was small, but nobody gave evidence suggesting otherwise. Harvey said his wife had gone to bed around two-thirty, but he'd poured himself another drink, fell asleep in the lounge. Two hours later he went down to their cabin – and no sign of Barbara Turner. He raised the alarm, a search of the boat followed and not long after came the call to the coastguard.'

'No one saw her fall?'

'No, her body washed up twenty-four hours later.'

'And the autopsy?'

'High levels of blood-alcohol, but no surprise there. Her lungs were filled with water, which might suggest she was still breathing when she went overboard, but after more than twenty-four hours in the ocean her lungs would fill naturally. Verdict given as accidental death by drowning.'

'Any luck with the passenger list?'

'Barbara Turner and Harvey Rylands, along with three members of crew and Mrs Turner's personal assistant. A woman called Amelia Madison.'

CHAPTER 28

'MADISON!' ROSCOE PUSHED HIS chair back from his desk and jumped to his feet. 'Josh, I owe you a beer!'

Disconnecting the line and grabbing a camera from his desk, Roscoe ran out of the control room and sprinted up the two flights of stairs to the entrance level of the hotel. Crossing the foyer, he caught Anna's eye as she welcomed two new guests to the hotel, and he enjoyed the look she gave him as he ran out through the front of the building.

Heading down the driveway, he could see Stanley standing at the front gate.

'Stanley,' called Roscoe, as he approached his assistant. 'What did you do with Michael Madison?'

'Deposited him on the roadside,' said Stanley, gesturing towards the media throng still gathered outside the hotel grounds. 'My guess is he's still hurting. You hit him pretty good.'

'I hope I haven't scared him off,' said Roscoe, looking out into the huge melee of journalists and television crews.

'Sorry, Boss?'

'I need to speak to him again. You think he's still around?'

'He'll still be hanging round alright – he's that type. Even with a smack on the jaw and cracked fingers, he doesn't know when he's beaten.'

'I have a feeling he might have more to tell us. I need to speak to him – fast.'

Stanley indicated to the guard to raise the newly installed security barrier and headed out into the street outside the hotel. Walking alongside him, Roscoe was astonished by size of the media city, as press people took phone calls and television journalists talked into cameras.

'Verdict's in, Jon,' said Stanley above the noise.

'And?'

'Guilty on all charges. I'm afraid it's new accommodation for Mr Rylands tonight. No further need for his suite on the fourteenth floor,' Stanley laughed. 'He's got some nice alternative housing waiting for him.'

'Let's hope he got what he deserves,' said Roscoe, as they crossed the road towards the royal park.

Stanley pointed ahead of them. 'Over there, Boss,' he said. 'Sharing his war stories with one of his comrades.'

'Thanks. If any more news from the Old Bailey comes through, let me have it,' said Roscoe.

He could see Madison sitting on the edge of the road, telling his story to another journalist. As he approached, Madison looked up.

'Leave me alone,' said Madison, still holding his jaw.

'Is this what you call Tribeca luxury service?' said the other journalist. 'You nearly killed him. He was only trying to do his job.'

'Is that right?' said Roscoe. 'And did he tell you how he kidnapped a seven-year-old girl and took her alone into one of the hotel suites?'

'Really?' said the journalist, looking first at Roscoe and then at Madison.

'Yes, really,' said Roscoe. 'So why don't take your misplaced sympathy, go across the road and join your fellow predators, to see what fresh prey you can hunt down.'

As the journalist stood up and walked away, Madison looked up at Roscoe.

'That wasn't fair. You know it wasn't like that with the girl.'

'I know, I'm sorry, but I need to talk to you alone,' said Roscoe, dropping the camera he had picked up from his desk into Madison's arms and taking a seat next to him on the kerb. 'I'm guessing that's yours?'

'Would have been one for you to put up on your living-room wall – nice picture of you and the Prime Minister.'

'Guess I'll have to live without that.'

'What do you want to talk to me about, anyway?' said Madison.

Roscoe knew he was the last person in the world the South African would want to speak to.

'Tell me about Amelia Madison.'

Surprised, Madison turned to look at Roscoe. 'I didn't think you'd be the one to ask me about her.'

'No?'

'I thought it would be one of that lot,' said Madison, looking across at the world's media.

'Why?'

'Because right now this is the biggest story in the world, and I thought someone might have had the brains to ask me about my part in it.'

'But they didn't?'

'You're the first,' said Madison, with an ironic laugh. 'Right now, everyone is talking about Harvey and the Prime Minister. I'm a footnote, lost somewhere in the dim-and-distant past, and that suits me just fine.'

'A footnote in what way?' asked Roscoe, knowing this had to come from Madison, to confirm his own growing suspicions.

Madison rubbed his jaw and sighed.

'As Amelia's first husband, of course.'

CHAPTER 29

INVISIBLE TO THOSE AROUND them, Roscoe and Madison remained seated on the roadside.

'I wasn't long out of school, travelling, working different jobs, not much more than a kid,' explained Madison, sharing his life story in a way neither he nor Roscoe could have imagined earlier in the day. 'Found myself drinking in a bar in Sydney with a load of Aussies, and Amelia was the girl bringing us beers. I remember us heading out that night after the bar closed, and her telling me she had no intention of spending the rest of her life waiting on other people. She was better than that, she said, she was going to have the best of everything, and in time people would be waiting on her. Whatever it took, that's what she'd have. We laughed about it at the time. I had no idea how much she meant it.'

Madison paused and looked over at his excited media colleagues, who were anticipating Amelia's return to the hotel.

'Go on,' said Roscoe.

'We started dating and I decided to stay. Got myself a job as a researcher for a local TV station in Sydney. Amelia quit the bar, became assistant to the Chief Exec of a big shipping company. Soon after I moved on to the written press, and we got ourselves a nice apartment on the edge of the city. We were set.'

Roscoe could see Madison was reluctant to say any more.

'And then what? I need to know, Michael,' he pushed.

Madison turned away. 'Amelia got pregnant. We were happy, or I thought we were. It was all I really wanted, but not Amelia. She came home one day and told me the baby was gone. I knew what she'd done.'

'I'm sorry,' said Roscoe, thinking of the joy his own kids brought to him.

'After that I guess it was only a matter of time until we went our separate ways, but I never imagined . . .'

'What happened?'

Madison turned back to Roscoe.

'Amelia was offered a job working for Barbara Turner. Her company had used the shipping company Amelia worked for, and they'd been introduced at some charity fundraiser. Very quickly all I heard was "Barbara said this", "Barbara said that". Amelia couldn't get enough of Barbara Turner, went everywhere with her, was dazzled by her. She had exactly what Amelia wanted – money, beautiful homes, fast cars, her own yacht.'

'And now Amelia's got all of them,' said Roscoe.

Madison shrugged.

'It wasn't too long before the stories changed from "Barbara and I did this deal" or "Barbara and I met this businessman" to "Harvey and I played tennis", "Harvey and I went for lunch at the marina", "Harvey is such fun". Suddenly Harvey was the smart one.' He paused. 'I knew then . . .'

'That they were having an affair?'

'One of Harvey's many. Except Amelia was different – a few nice gifts weren't going to cut it. She wanted the lot.'

'And she got it.'

'Indeed. Three weeks after Barbara's death she came to me and said she planned to marry Harvey and wanted a quick, uncontested divorce.'

'She must have decided to reel him in while she had the chance,' Roscoe said, certain that Amelia could be exceptionally persuasive when she wanted to be.

'With the sweetener of a two-million dollar payment to me, I wasn't going to stand in their way.'

'Wow!' exclaimed Roscoe.

'I know.'

'Blood-money?'

'At the time I didn't think so. Amelia was on the yacht the night Barbara died, but she seemed genuinely cut up about what happened.'

'Cut up for three weeks, until she offered you two million dollars for a divorce?'

Madison laughed.

'When I saw the reports of the attack on Elegant Daniels, my gut told me something was wrong. She was another woman who was close to Harvey: a challenge to Amelia.'

Roscoe pulled the divorce papers out of his pocket and passed them to Madison.

'Your gut was right – something is very wrong. You were looking in the right place and, with a bit more luck, you'd have found these.'

Madison read the papers and whistled in surprise. 'Barbara was going to divorce him? That would have left Harvey with nothing.'

'What do you mean?'

'Barbara's fortune was very well protected. Her mother had been the real brains, having built the business from nothing. She was absolutely dedicated to it. From what I remember, she didn't have Barbara until she was in her mid-forties and not long after that she divorced her husband, who went off to sire your current Prime Minister. Barbara was raised by a single mother. That meant going into the office most days, travelling the world together and Barbara learning how deals were done. It was a great education for her. The only falling-out between mother and daughter came over Barbara's plan to marry Harvey – a playboy who came with a wild reputation. Mother refused to hand the company over to her daughter unless the tightest of pre-nups was in place – meaning that Harvey would get not a penny more, not a penny less than one hundred thousand dollars if the marriage ever failed.'

'But instead he inherited . . . ?'

'Close to a billion dollars.'

CHAPTER 30

WHEN THE JURY DELIVERED its verdict, a torrent of emotion swept across Amelia Rylands.

A torrent of pure, unadulterated pleasure.

She continued looking straight ahead at the judge, not for one second turning to look at her husband as he was led away from the court.

As soon as the opportunity allowed, she quickly left the Old Bailey, jumped into her waiting sports car and drove herself back to the Tribeca Luxury Hotel.

Reversing the car into a space close to the staff entrance, she briskly stepped out and walked through the hotel to ride the elevator to the fourteenth floor.

She was elated.

In her heart she knew Harvey would never have achieved anything without her.

Who had planned the killing of Barbara Turner?

Not Harvey.

He didn't have the strength.

But she had given him her strength.

She gave him everything.

And then he'd betrayed her.

How dare he tell her that he was leaving?

Leaving her with nothing.

Discarding her.

And for no more than a dirty hooker.

Standing in the elevator, Amelia's face broke out into the broadest smile.

She had won.

As she walked down the hall, Amelia congratulated herself on committing the perfect crime.

Attacking Elegant Daniels in her bed, smothering her in the exact same way Harvey had killed Barbara: the very plan she had devised for Harvey, re-enacted on his own precious whore twenty years later.

The delicious irony being that Harvey was the only person who knew of her guilt – and the one person who could never accuse her.

How she revelled in Harvey knowing it was her; and in his needing her to play the loyal wife, if he ever hoped to be acquitted.

He needed her.

Like he always had.

He was nothing without her.

And dressing the whore with the rubies? She liked to think of them as her calling card – so Harvey was never in any doubt who had attacked Elegant.

And then Elegant lived – which felt like an added bonus. It was her performance as a lover spurned that had sent Harvey down.

It was too late for him to say anything now. It would sound like the ravings of a bitter convict.

Euphoric, Amelia walked into her suite.

It was all hers.

She headed straight to the bathroom where she kept her insurance, in case of an acquittal: the divorce petition, the keeper of Harvey's guilt, from so many years before. Of course, as Barbara's personal assistant, she had access to even her most private of papers.

And the other rubies? They were nothing more than meaningless gifts from Harvey. She would have used them on him, just as she did on his whore.

But as she stepped into the bathroom, she saw her vanity case had been moved.

Her insurance was gone.

CHAPTER 31

NOW WAS NOT THE time to panic, Amelia told herself.

Remember: she had won.

In less than an hour she would be safely on board Harvey's private jet.

Her private jet.

She had to act fast. Someone in the hotel had discovered the divorce papers. In as calm a manner as possible, she needed to leave immediately.

Don't let it slip away. She was almost there.

Suddenly racked with nerves, she took the elevator down through the hotel. A confident walk through the foyer was all that was required.

No one could suspect her.

Her body mustn't betray her.

Weakness was unforgivable.

A confident walk, accompanied by an air of inaccessibility, was what she needed to convey.

My husband has been convicted – don't try to console me.

As the elevator doors opened, Amelia stepped into the vast marble foyer.

And stopped.

Astonished.

A double take.

Michael, her husband from another life, speaking to the Head of Security. Where had he come from? Why now? She hadn't seen him in over twenty years.

Momentarily she was dazed.

She told herself to regain her composure, but that one second of faltering was all it took.

Roscoe had seen her.

Roscoe had seen her.

He watched Amelia waver, before she hurriedly exited the elevator.

She was fleeing through the back of the hotel.

'I need you to find Stanley,' he instructed Madison. 'Tell him I'm following Amelia out through the back. Get him to call the police and then to head out the front gate. I'll follow her round, and we can cut her off.'

Roscoe quickly followed Amelia as she made her way through the restaurant and into the kitchen.

He had to stop her.

She was as guilty as Harvey, Roscoe was certain of that.

And the rubies told him she was guilty of a whole lot more.

He knew a moment's hesitation running through the kitchen and he would have her.

She knew a moment's hesitation running through the kitchen and he would have her.

Skipping from side to side, avoiding the waiters, Amelia looked over her shoulder to see Roscoe quickening his pace.

'Get out of my way,' she screamed, as she relished the chase. Sprinting now, this was her race to the line.

Win this and she was free.

She bolted out of the rear of the hotel, the door flying open as she charged through into the parking lot.

Her car was in sight.

As she clicked the keys on her tiny sports car, the lights flashed.

The second she was in, the engine fired.

He was exiting the back of the hotel, but she was away.

He couldn't catch her now.

As he ran towards her, she raced the car forward.

She was driving directly at him.

CHAPTER 32

SHE WAS DRIVING DIRECTLY at him.

He could see her manic eyes as she clutched the steering wheel, unyielding in her attack.

In an act of self-preservation, Roscoe threw himself to the ground, rolling forward, desperately trying to take cover behind a Tribeca vehicle.

Her car continued its forward momentum, veering to the side at the last moment to avoid a head-on collision. Swerving, she clipped the front of the Tribeca car, before accelerating away towards the exit.

Scrambling to his feet, Roscoe jumped into his car and, without a second's hesitation, continued the pursuit.

Hitting the accelerator, he rapidly increased his speed through the parking lot. Looking ahead at her racing down the exit ramp, he could see the barrier was down.

*

Looking ahead, racing down the exit ramp, she could see the barrier was down.

Squeezing harder on the accelerator, she closed her eyes, feeling the car rise upwards as she tore straight through the barricade. Slamming to the ground with a crash, she spun a hard left, her tyres screeching as she hit the side road.

Oblivious to oncoming traffic, she accelerated again, turning onto the main road in front of the hotel. In a blur she saw a runner standing frozen, crossing from the royal park.

She didn't care.

This was her war.

And war had casualties.

She was going to hit the runner.

She was going to hit the runner.

Roscoe could see it all.

Instantly he knew.

The runner was Martin.

His heart hammering in his chest, he pushed the high-powered SUV engine to its max.

Pulling alongside, he looked directly at her.

Her face possessed by greed, she never flinched.

He knew he had no choice. It was her or his son.

He turned his car directly into hers.

CHAPTER 33

AMELIA RYLANDS' SPORTS CONVERTIBLE twisted skywards, before smashing into the towering stone wall that surrounds London's Tribeca Luxury Hotel. Falling back to earth, it speared itself onto the hood of Roscoe's SUV, before crumpling to the ground.

The media throng divided equally between those seeking cover and those wanting to secure the final desperate picture in the Harvey and Amelia Rylands saga.

Pushing open his car door, Roscoe ran straight across to Martin, who stood ashen-faced and motionless in the middle of the road. Putting his arms around his son and holding him tightly, he said, 'Maybe next time you'll listen to your dad when he says don't run on the road wearing headphones.'

Still in shock, Martin said nothing, burying his head into his dad's chest.

Continuing to hold onto his son tightly, Roscoe watched as Stanley walked from the front gate of the hotel, along the road to Amelia Rylands' car. Finding her impaled through the throat by the steering column, her head almost severed, Stanley simply looked across at Roscoe and shook his head.

With his arm still tight around his son's shoulder, Roscoe slowly stepped through the media scrum, ignoring the photographers' flashing cameras, and headed up the driveway to the front of the hotel.

'So, you going to tell me why you were out running on your own?' asked Roscoe, halfway up the drive.

'Dad, I'm sorry,' said Martin hesitantly, stopping to face his father. 'I quit the track team.'

'If I know you, it'll be for a good reason,' said Roscoe.

'Coach Davis. He wants us to win at all costs.' Martin paused for a moment. 'He's been pressuring some of us to take steroids. He never quite made it on the track himself, so now he's desperate to be the coach of a national champion. He doesn't care what he has to do to get it. I threatened to report him. And then I quit the team. I'm sorry I lied to you, Dad.'

'I couldn't be more proud of you,' Roscoe said, pulling his son close.

CHAPTER 34

THE ESPRESSO BAR AT the Tribeca Luxury Hotel in the Mayfair district of London serves some of the best coffee available in the capital city. Courtesy of Jessie Luck's Auntie's Bakery, it also serves the very best baked goods money can buy.

Sitting with Martin and Anna, Roscoe tried not to think about how close he came to losing his son but, as he savoured his coffee and watched Martin devour a chocolate brownie, he gave thanks for the wonderful young man he had done his very best to raise over the past fifteen years.

'So, Dad, if Amelia Rylands already had more money than she could ever hope to spend, why did she try to kill Elegant Daniels?'

'Because Elegant was a threat,' said Anna.

'Exactly,' said Roscoe. 'A threat to everything Amelia felt she had worked so hard to achieve; a threat to her wealth, to her status.'

'But why?' asked Martin, helping himself to another brownie.

'Over twenty years ago, Harvey Rylands and Amelia Madison killed his first wife, Barbara Turner. I don't know exactly how, but if I'm guessing, Harvey suffocated her in her own bed while they were sailing around the Great Barrier Reef. Once he'd killed her, he and Amelia dumped the body overboard. It was an easy step from there to say she had drunk too much and drowned.'

'Once that was done,' said Anna, 'Harvey was free to marry Amelia.'

'I bet Michael Madison got dumped real quick,' Martin said. 'He must have felt pretty sore – but not as sore as when you knocked him out, Dad!'

'A couple of million dollars softened the blow,' said Roscoe, 'and at least today he helped get the answers he's been looking for, even if his jaw is a little tender.'

'But why kill Elegant Daniels?' asked Martin. 'Wasn't she just another one of Harvey's women?'

'Yes and no,' said Roscoe. 'It must have started like that. Harvey was introduced to her by the Prime Minister, who was probably looking for an easy way to slow down his own relationship. But Harvey broke Amelia's golden rule.'

'"Don't fall in love,"' said Anna. 'It was fine for Harvey to have all the women in the world, as long as at the end of the day he came home to Amelia.'

'And once Harvey had told Amelia he planned to leave her for Elegant, Elegant's days were numbered,' continued Roscoe. 'Who else could have found such easy access to Elegant's house and to Harvey's car? Nobody – except Harvey's wife. Amelia was determined no one was going to take the Rylands fortune away from her.'

'Do you think Elegant genuinely thought Harvey had attacked her?' asked Anna.

Roscoe shrugged. 'We can't be sure. But she was angry – angry at Harvey, angry at the world. So she decided to use her appearance in court to take her revenge.'

'And why did Amelia leave the rubies at the scene?' asked Martin.

'Sheer hatred. And she needed to be certain Harvey knew who had carried out the attack.'

'Because there was nothing he could do about it?' said Anna.

'Nothing,' said Roscoe. 'They were rubies from the very mine Harvey had inherited after killing his first wife, in the very same way, twenty years before.'

'So, Dad,' said Martin, considering the evidence, 'Harvey's in prison for a crime he didn't commit?'

Roscoe smiled at his son.

'It's a funny thing, justice. He wasn't directly responsible for attacking Elegant Daniels, but it all stemmed from the murder he did commit many years before – a murder it's impossible to prove. I think it's time he served his sentence.'

CHAPTER 35

ROSCOE WAS LOOKING FORWARD to a weekend in Scotland with his two daughters, Aimee and Lauren, but he had one stop to make before he hit the road north.

Pulling through the gates of Martin's school, he listened on news radio to a statement from the Prime Minister that, for family reasons, he was announcing his resignation with immediate effect.

He left his car at the edge of the sports field and walked across the damp grass to where Coach Davis was training with a group of teenage kids.

Seeing Roscoe approaching, Coach Davis walked in his direction. As the father of one of the school's star athletes, Roscoe was known by the coach, who offered his hand in greeting. Ignoring him, Roscoe took one step forward and, with a single punch, knocked the coach to the ground, relishing the sound of breaking the man's jaw as he fell.

Blood was running from Coach Davis' mouth as Roscoe knelt beside him.

'Push drugs on kids again and next time, I promise, I will kill you.'

He stood up and towered over the floored man lying prone on the ground.

'And, Coach Davis,' said Roscoe, 'I expect to hear by the end of the day that the Prime Minister is not the only man who has announced his resignation with immediate effect.'

Molly Rourke's son has been murdered . . . and she
knows who's responsible.

Read on for an extract

A MOTHER'S INSTINCT to protect her child—the most powerful force on the planet.

Right now I'm bursting with it. Overwhelmed by it. Trembling from it.

My son, my precious little boy, is hurt. Or, God forbid, it's worse.

I don't know the details of what's happened. I don't even know where he is.

I just know I have to save him.

I slam on the brakes. The tires of my old Dodge Ram screech like hell. One of them pops the curb, jerking me forward hard against the wheel. But I'm so numb with fear and panic, I barely feel the impact.

I grab the door handle—but stop and count to three. I force myself to take three deep breaths. I make the sign of the cross: three times again.

And I pray that I find my son fast—*in three minutes or less.*

I leap out and start running. The fastest I've ever moved in my life.

Oh, Alex. What have you done?

He's such a good kid. Such a smart kid. A tough kid, too—especially with all our family's been going through. I'm not a perfect mother. But I've always done the best I know how. Alex isn't perfect, either, but I love him more than anything. And I'm so proud of him, so proud of the young man he's becoming before my eyes.

I just want to see him again—*safe*. And I'd give anything for it. *Anything.*

I reach the two-story brick building's front doors. Above them hangs a faded green-and-white banner I must have read a thousand times:

HOBART HIGH SCHOOL—HOME OF THE RAIDERS

Could be any other high school in America. Certainly any in sweltering west Texas. But somewhere inside is my son. And goddamnit, I'm coming for him.

I burst through the doors—*But where the hell am I going?*

I've spent more hours in this building than I could ever count. Hell, I graduated from this school nearly twenty years ago. But suddenly, the layout feels strange to me. Foreign.

I start running down the central hallway. Terrified. Desperate. Frenzied.

Oh, Alex. At fifteen, he's still just a child. He loves comic books—especially the classics like Batman and Spider-Man. He loves video games, the more frenzied the better. He loves being outdoors, too. Shooting and fishing especially. Riding his dirt bike—shiny blue, his favorite color—around abandoned oil fields with his friends.

But my son is also turning into an adult. He's been staying out later and later, especially on Fridays and Saturdays. He's started cruising around the county in his friends' cars. Just a few weeks ago—I didn't say anything, I was too shocked—but I smelled beer on his breath. The teenage years can be so hard. I remember my own rocky ones. I just hope I've raised him well enough to handle them....

"Alex!" I scream, my shrill voice echoing off the rows of metal lockers.

The text had come from Alex's cell phone—Miss Molly this is Danny—but it was written by his best friend since first grade. I always liked Danny. He came from a good family. But rumor was, he'd recently started making some bad choices. I'd been secretly worrying he'd pressure Alex to make the same ones someday.

The moment I read that text, I knew he had.

Alex did too much. Not breathing. At school come fast.

Next thing I remember, I'm in my truck roaring down Route 84, dialing Alex's cell, cursing when neither of them answers. I call his principal. I call my brothers. I call 911.

And then I pray: I call in a favor from God.

"Alex!" I yell again, even louder, to no one and everyone. "Where are you?!"

But the students I pass now just gawk. Some point and

snicker. Others point and click, snapping cell-phone pictures of the crazy lady running wild through their school.

Don't they know what's happening?! How can they be like this, so...

Wait. Teenagers spread rumors faster than a brushfire, and it's way too quiet. Maybe they *don't* know.

He must be on the second floor.

I head to the nearest stairway and pound up the steps. My lungs start to burn and my heart races. At the top, the hallway forks.

Damn it, which way, where is he?!

Something tells me to hang a left. Maybe a mother's intuition. Maybe blind, stupid luck. Either way, I listen.

There, down at the end, a growing crowd is gathering outside the boys' bathroom. Kids and teachers. Some yelling. Some crying. All panicking.

Like I am.

"I'm his mother!" I push and shove toward the middle. "Move! Out of my way!"

I spot Alex's legs first, splayed out limp and crooked. I see his scuffed-up Converses, the soles wrapped in duct tape, apparently some kind of fashion trend. I recognize the ratty old pair of Levi's he wore at breakfast this morning, the ones I sewed a new patch onto last week. I can make out a colorful rolled-up comic book jutting out of the back pocket.

And then I see his right arm, outstretched on the ground.

His lifeless fingers clutching a small glass pipe, its round tip charred and black.

Oh, Alex, how could you do this?

His homeroom teacher, the school nurse, and a fit youngish man I don't recognize wearing a HHS baseball T-shirt are all hunched over his body, frantically performing CPR.

But *I'm* the one who's just stopped breathing.

"No, no, no…Alex! My poor baby…"

How did this happen? How did I let it? How could I have been so blind?

My knees start to buckle. My head gets light. My vision spins. I start to lose my balance….

"Molly, easy now, we got ya."

I feel four sturdy hands grab me from behind: Stevie and Hank, the best big brothers a girl could ask for. As soon as I called them to say what had happened, they rushed right over to the high school. They're my two rocks. Who I need now more than ever.

"He's gonna be all right," Hank whispers. "Everything's gonna be fine."

I know he's just saying that—but they're words I desperately need to hear and believe. I don't have the strength, or the will, to respond.

I let him and Stevie hold me steady. I can't move a muscle. Can't take my eyes off Alex, either. He looks so thin, so weak. So young. So vulnerable. His skin pale as Xerox paper. His lips flecked with frothy spittle. His eyes like sunken glass orbs.

"Who sold him that shit?!"

Stevie spins to face the crowd, spewing white-hot rage. His voice booms across the hallway. "Who did this?! Who?!"

The crowd instantly falls silent. A retired Marine, Stevie is that damn scary. Not a sound can be heard—except for the wail of an ambulance siren.

"Somebody better talk to me! Now!"

Yet no one makes a peep. No one dares to.

But no one *needs* to.

Because as I watch the last drops of life drain from Alex's body, my own life changed and dimmed forever, I realize I already know the answer.

I know who killed my son.

THE OLD JEEP rattles slowly down the long dusty road, like a cheetah stalking its prey. A symphony of crickets fills the hot night air. A passing train whistles off in the distance. A pale sliver of moon, the only light for miles.

Gripping the steering wheel is Stevie Rourke. His eyes gaze straight ahead. A former staff sergeant in the United States Marine Corps, he's forty-four years old, six feet six inches tall, and 249 pounds of solid muscle. A man so loyal to his friends and family, he'd rush the gates of hell for them, and wrestle the devil himself.

Hank Rourke, trim and wiry, younger by only a few years, with a similar devotion but a far shorter fuse, is sitting shotgun—and loading shells into one, too.

"We're less than 180 seconds out," Stevie says.

Hank grunts in understanding.

The two brothers ride in tense silence for the rest of the brief trip. No words needed. They've discussed their plan and know exactly what they're going to do.

Confront the good-for-nothing son of a bitch who killed their fifteen-year-old nephew.

Stevie and Hank both loved that boy. Loved him as if he were their own son. And Alex loved them both back. Molly's worthless drunk of a husband had taken off when the boy was just a baby. But no one had shed any tears. Not then, not since. Molly reclaimed her maiden name for her and Alex. The whole Rourke family was already living together on their big family farm, and with no children of their own, Hank and Stevie stepped right up. The void left by one lousy father was filled by two incredible uncles. And Alex's life was all the better for it.

Until today. When his life came to a heartbreaking end.

Both brothers dropped everything as soon as Molly called them. They drove together straight to the high school, their truck rattling along at over a hundred miles per hour. They were hoping for the best....

But had prepared themselves for the worst.

The doctors and sheriff's department are treating Alex's death as an accident. At least for now. Just two kids being kids, messing with shit they shouldn't have been.

But it was an accident that didn't have to happen.

And somebody is going to pay.

Their destination soon comes into sight: a cluster of low-slung wood and metal buildings that seem to shimmer in the still-scorching desert heat. Hank surveys the area with a pair of forest-green binoculars.

"Don't see anyone on patrol. Maybe we can sneak up on him after all."

Stevie shakes his head.

"That bastard knows we're coming."

The Jeep comes to a stop in front of a rusty padlocked gate on the perimeter of the property, dotted with dry shrubs and scraggly trees. At the end of a short driveway sits a tumble-down little shack.

The man they've come for lives inside.

Stuffing his Glock 19 into his belt behind his back, Stevie steps out of the Jeep first—and the blistering desert air hits him like a semi. Instantly he's flooded with memories of the nighttime covert ops he ran in Desert Storm. But that was a distant land, where more than two decades earlier he served with honor and distinction.

Tonight, he's in Scurry County, Texas. He doesn't have an elite squad to back him up. Only his jumpy little brother.

And the stakes aren't just higher. They're personal.

"Lay a hand on my gate, Rourke, I'll blow it clean off."

Old Abe McKinley is standing on his farmhouse porch, shakily aiming a giant wood-handled Colt Anaconda. With his wild mane of white hair and blackened teeth, he either looks awful for seventy-five, or like total shit for sixty.

But Stevie doesn't scare easy—or back down.

"I want to talk to you, Abe. Nothing more."

"Then tell your baby brother to be smart. And put down his toy."

"If you tell your folks to do the same."

Abe snorts. *Not a chance.*

Stevie shrugs. Worth a try. "Then at least tell 'em," he says, "to quit pretending to hide."

After a reluctant nod from the old man, Hank tosses his pump-action Remington back into the Jeep. Simultaneously, fourteen of McKinley's goons, hidden all around the compound, slowly step out of the shadows. Some were crouched behind bushes. Others, trees. A few were lying prone in the knee-high grass that covers most of McKinley's two dozen acres.

Each man is wearing full hunting camo and a ski mask, and clutching a semiautomatic weapon.

Stevie was right. The bastard sure *did* know they'd be coming around here.

"Now, then." Stevie clears his throat. "As I was saying—"

"Sorry to hear about your sister's boy." McKinley interrupts. Not one for small talk. He spits a thick squirt of tobacco juice into the dirt. "Tragedy."

Stevie swallows his rage at the intentional sign of complete disrespect. "You sound real cut up about it. *About losing a first-time customer.*"

McKinley betrays nothing. "I don't know what you mean by that. If you're implying I had anything to do with—"

Hank's the one who interrupts now. Can't keep his cool like his brother.

"You got four counties hooked on the crystal you cook!"

he shouts, taking a step forward. McKinley's men raise their guns, but Hank doesn't flinch.

"You're the biggest player from here to Lubbock, and everybody knows it. Means one of y'all"—Hank glares at each of the armed men, one by one, their fingers tickling their triggers—"sold our nephew the shit that killed him. Put a live grenade in the hand of a child!"

McKinley just snarls. Then turns and starts heading back inside his house.

"Stevie, Hank, thanks for stopping by. But don't do it again. Or I'll bury you out back with the dogs."

Like a shot from a rifle—*crack!*—the screen door slams shut behind him.

TOMORROW MARKS TEN weeks to the day my son Alex died before my eyes.

I can't believe it. It feels like barely ten minutes.

I can still remember so clearly the pair of fresh-faced paramedics who rushed into the hallway and lifted him onto a gurney. I remember the breakneck ambulance ride to the county hospital, all those machines he was hooked up to, clicking and beeping, me clutching his clammy hand, urging him to hang on to his life just as tight.

I remember when we arrived and the EMTs slid out his stretcher, I saw the comic book Alex had in his back pocket. It got jostled and fluttered to the ground. As he was wheeled away into the ER, I stopped to scoop it up, and then frantically ran after them.

I screamed and waved it in the air like a madman, as if they were army medics carrying a blast victim off a battlefield and had left behind his missing limb. Of course I wasn't thinking straight. How could any mother at a time like that? I kept wailing and bawling until finally one of the nurses took hold of those few dozen colorful pages and promised to give them to my son.

"When he wakes up!" I said, both my hands on her shoulders. "Please!"

The nurse nodded. And smiled sadly. "Of course, ma'am. When he wakes up."

Two days later, that crinkled comic book was returned to me.

It came in a sealed plastic bag that also held my son's wallet, cell phone, and the clothes he was wearing when he was admitted, including his Converses wrapped in duct tape and his old pair of Levi's.

Alex never woke up.

My brother Hank suddenly jars me out of my dazed memory—by punching the kitchen wall with his meaty fist so hard, the framed pictures and hanging decorative plates all rattle. He's always been the hotheaded one. The firecracker in the family. Tonight is no different.

"The Rourkes have owned this land for three generations!" he shouts. "No goddamn way we're gonna lose it to the bank in three months!"

Before any of us can respond, he punches the wall again— even harder—and an antique piece of china that belonged to our late grandmother Esther Rourke slips off its holder and smashes into pieces.

Debbie, Hank's bubbly blond wife, gasps in horror. But I

couldn't care less. It's just a thing. An object. Sure, it had been in our family for years, but today our family itself is shattered. My *heart* is shattered. Who cares if some stupid old plate is, too? In fact, I'm happy to clean it up. Happy for a distraction from all the yelling and cursing and arguing of the past hour—which I hope we can wrap up in a few more minutes.

But before I can fetch a broom, Stevie takes my shoulder.

"Walk us through it one more time, Molly," he says. "It's one hell of a plan."

I can't deny that. On the surface, it sounds reckless. Crazy. Nearly impossible.

But I've had plenty of time to think over every last detail. And I believe with every piece of my broken heart that we can do it.

We *have* to do it.

See, well before Alex passed, the bank had been calling—sometimes twice, three times a day. The notices were piling up. Stevie, Hank, their wives, and me, we all scrimped as best we could. Even Alex, my big man, my baby, had been handing over the crumpled five-dollar bills he earned mowing Mrs. Baker's lawn down the road.

But it wasn't enough. The payments, the interest—I knew we'd never be able to cover it all. We'd keep slipping further and further behind. I knew it was only a matter of time before we lost our home for good.

And then, we were faced with a totally unexpected additional expense, which sped the process up even more.

The cost of my only child's funeral.

So now, in just ninety days, the ten-acre farm our family has called home for so long will become the legal property of First Texas Credit Union. Unless we put my "hell of a plan," the one I'd been mulling over for months, into action.

And, by the grace of God, pull it off.

"Save your breath," Hank says to me. "It's madness, Molly. Pure and simple."

Again I can't deny that. At least under normal circumstances, I can't.

"Desperate times," says Stevie's wife, Kim, with a quiet intensity. A military daughter and spouse, she's a wise brunette beauty, no stranger to hard choices. Over the last twelve years that she's been married to my oldest brother, she's become the sister I never had. When it became clear that children of their own weren't in the cards, she could have gotten resentful. Bitter. Instead, Kim directed all that excess love toward Alex. She was the only one of us, for example, who had the patience to teach him to ride a bike, a hobby he kept up until his last days.

"I wanna know what *he* thinks," Hank fires back, pointing at the man who's been sitting in the adjacent dining room, sipping iced sweet tea with lemon, listening patiently this whole time, barely uttering a word. "If *he* says it's crazy, you *know* it's gotta be—"

"Doesn't matter," I say. "This is family-only. Either we're all in, or we're all out. Right on our asses, too."

My brothers and sisters-in-law chew on that. So do Nick

and J.D., two retired Marines Stevie served with in the Middle East so long ago, who became as close as blood. Especially in recent years, they'd become like big brothers to Alex, taking him on hunting and fishing trips for some critical male bonding. They were in the second row at his funeral, two burly ex-soldiers dabbing at their eyes.

I explain one final time exactly what I'm proposing. My plan is a long haul with short odds. It might cost us everything. But doing nothing *definitely* would.

After a tense silence that feels like it goes on forever…

"In," Stevie says simply. Marines don't mince their words.

"*Semper fi,*" says Nick, stepping forward. He and J.D. both give stiff salutes.

Kim clasps her husband's hand. "That makes four, then."

Debbie nervously twirls her yellow locks, blinking, unsure. I like Debbie—or, should I say, I've *grown* to like her. We probably wouldn't be friends if she weren't married to my brother. Debbie's sweet, but timid. Tries a little too hard to please. She'd rather go with the flow than rock the boat, especially when her husband's in it. She looks to Hank for guidance; she doesn't get it. So she does something surprising. She goes with her gut.

"This place, after all these years…it's become *my* home, too. I'll do it."

Hank throws up his hands. He's the final holdout.

"You're asking me to pick my family or my conscience. You understand that?"

My eyes flutter to a framed, faded photograph on the wall of Alex at age six. He's sitting in a tire swing hanging from the branch of a giant oak tree on our farm, smiling a gap-toothed grin. He looks so little. So happy. So innocent.

So alive.

"Sounds like an easy choice to me," I say.

At last, with a heavy sigh, Hank nods. He's in, too.

And so the vote is unanimous. *My plan is a go.*

"Just one little problem," Debbie says nervously, bending down now to pick up the pieces of the antique plate her husband broke.

"Where are we gonna get seventy-five grand to pull this thing off?"

JAMES PATTERSON

BOOK**SHOTS**

OUT THIS MONTH

113 MINUTES

Molly Rourke's son has been murdered . . . and she knows who's responsible. Now she's taking the law into her own hands.

THE VERDICT

A billionaire businessman is on trial for violently attacking a woman in her bed. No one is prepared for the terrifying consequences of the verdict.

THE MATING SEASON

Sophie Castle has been given the opportunity of a lifetime: her own wildlife documentary. But her cameraman, Rigg Greensman, is unmotivated . . . and drop dead gorgeous.

TRUMP VS. CLINTON: IN THEIR OWN WORDS (ebook only)

Direct from the candidates, *Trump vs. Clinton* is an unvarnished conversation on the issues in this dramatic presidential election.

JAMES PATTERSON
BOOKSHOTS
COMING SOON

FRENCH KISS

French detective Luc Moncrief joined the NYPD for a fresh start – but someone wants to make his first big case his last.

$10,000,000 MARRIAGE PROPOSAL

A billboard offering $10 million to get married intrigues three single women in LA. But who is Mr. Right . . . and is he the perfect match for the lucky winner?

SACKING THE QUARTERBACK

Attorney Melissa St. James wins every case. Now, when she's up against football superstar Grayson Knight, her heart is on the line, too.

KILL OR BE KILLED

Four gripping thrillers – one killer collection. *The Trial, Little Black Dress, Heist* and *The Women's War*.

THE WOMEN'S WAR (ebook only)

Former Marine Corps colonel Amanda Collins and her lethal team of women warriors have vowed to avenge her family's murder.

BOOKSHOTS

STORIES AT THE SPEED OF LIFE

www.bookshots.com

ALSO BY JAMES PATTERSON

Private Down Under (*with Michael White*)
Private L.A. (*with Mark Sullivan*)
Private India (*with Ashwin Sanghi*)
Private Vegas (*with Maxine Paetro*)
Private Sydney (*with Kathryn Fox*)
Private Paris (*with Mark Sullivan*)
The Games (*with Mark Sullivan*)

NYPD RED SERIES
NYPD Red (*with Marshall Karp*)
NYPD Red 2 (*with Marshall Karp*)
NYPD Red 3 (*with Marshall Karp*)
NYPD Red 4 (*with Marshall Karp*)

STAND-ALONE THRILLERS
Sail (*with Howard Roughan*)
Swimsuit (*with Maxine Paetro*)
Don't Blink (*with Howard Roughan*)
Postcard Killers (*with Liza Marklund*)
Toys (*with Neil McMahon*)
Now You See Her (*with Michael Ledwidge*)
Kill Me If You Can (*with Marshall Karp*)
Guilty Wives (*with David Ellis*)
Zoo (*with Michael Ledwidge*)
Second Honeymoon (*with Howard Roughan*)
Mistress (*with David Ellis*)
Invisible (*with David Ellis*)
The Thomas Berryman Number
Truth or Die (*with Howard Roughan*)
Murder House (*with David Ellis*)
Never Never (*with Candice Fox*)

NON-FICTION
Torn Apart (*with Hal and Cory Friedman*)
The Murder of King Tut (*with Martin Dugard*)

ROMANCE
Sundays at Tiffany's (*with Gabrielle Charbonnet*)
The Christmas Wedding (*with Richard DiLallo*)
First Love (*with Emily Raymond*)

OTHER TITLES
Miracle at Augusta (*with Peter de Jonge*)

BOOKSHOTS
Black & Blue (*with Candice Fox*)
Break Point (*with Lee Stone*)
Cross Kill
Private Royals (*with Rees Jones*)
The Hostage (*with Robert Gold*)
Zoo 2 (*with Max DiLallo*)
Heist (*with Rees Jones*)
Hunted (*with Andrew Holmes*)
Airport: Code Red (*with Michael White*)
The Trial (*with Maxine Paetro*)
Little Black Dress (*with Emily Raymond*)
Chase (*with Michael Ledwidge*)
Let's Play Make-Believe (*with James O. Born*)
Dead Heat (*with Lee Stone*)
Triple Threat